Haven

A Hate To Love Single Dad Romance

Keke Renée

Latest Releases

- Wet Heat (Wet Heat Series Book 1)
- Every Time We Touch Novelette (Wet Heat Book 2 Series)
- His Peace, Her Pleasure
- Baby, It's Cold Outside
- Love Don't Live Here Anymore, Vanessa Andrew Book 1
- Love Don't Live Here Anymore, Isabella Andrew Book 2
- One Night Only—A Novelette (Love by Design Book 1)
- Cassian and Savannah (Love by Design Book 2)
- Deidra's Love (Love by Design Book 3)
- Protecting Bria (Special Force Operation Alphas)
- Sensual: A Brother's Best Friend Romance
- Seek To Please Book 1
- Seek To Touch Book 2
- Seek To Bare Book 3
- Seek To Love Book 4

• Protecting Chanel (Special Forces Operation Alphas)

• Seek To Trust Book 5

• Seek To Earn Book 6

• Protecting Yanira (Special Forces Operation Alphas)

• Tease Me Book 1

• Please Me Book 2

First and foremost, I want to thank God for giving me the strength to keep pursuing my dreams and goals. My mom and big brother. My niece and nephew, and all my cousins. Especially a huge thanks to my family in heaven: Grandmother, Aunt, Father. You are always with me no matter where I go, and everything you taught me has made me a better person.

Introduction

Are you signed up for my newsletter?

Join today for all the latest new releases, contests, giveaways, sneak peeks, and more.

https://BookHip.com/BKRPJL

Author's note:

This story was originally a part of Samantha Cole's Suspenseful Shared World in 2020. Revised and Republished without those characters for 2023.

Synopsis

Dr. Kevin Haven needs a fresh start after losing his wife. His child is now his only concern, but when a new nurse arrives, she takes his world by storm, and it's all he can do to keep his emotions out of the situation. Not to mention the jealous women who will do anything to keep the new nurse from stealing the eligible bachelor's heart.

Nurse April Benson is no-nonsense and practical. She doesn't want or need a man for happiness. Life is all about her career and protecting herself from disappointment. So when Kevin captures her attention, she sets up ground rules, but the closer they get, the harder they are to follow.

Are Kevin and April ready for a real relationship, or are they headed for disaster?

Chapter 1

Kevin

It felt like yesterday when I held Aaliyah's hand as she gave birth to Ella. Now, here I was at thirty-three, a widower with a rambunctious six-year-old who kept me on my toes. She'd slowly begun to understand that her mom wasn't here anymore.

Aaliyah had been my best friend and wife. We'd known each other for over ten years. We'd dated for six and were married for four. She'd been a nurse, and I'd been an expert marksman in the Navy. I'd later gone into medicine and become a doctor, saving lives rather than taking them.

I'd needed a fresh start after Aaliyah died in a car accident a year ago. Leaving the fast pace of Los Angeles for Memphis had been a smooth transition, thanks to my friend, Warren. I'd met him through his wife, Kyla, when I assisted at Baptist Memorial Hospital while she battled cancer. We'd stayed in touch since she'd been in remission and had oncologist follow-up visits. We'd bonded over our kids, and it had helped that many of our friends were former military men.

Warren and Kyla had always ensured they included my daughter, Ella, in any activities. Warren had convinced me to start over in Tennessee, making it easy by letting me move into one of his properties—a four-bedroom, two-story house in a gated subdivision. I'd quickly transferred to Baptist Memorial Hospital as an Emergency Room Doctor, and the staff had become like family and friends.

Things had calmed down regarding taking care of Ella, getting her into a stable routine, and making friends.

My parents had moved here a few weeks ago. They'd decided to get a home in the same subdivision to be nearby and give Ella some normalcy. Aaliyah's parents, Marcia and Timothy, still lived in Los Angeles and had visited a few weeks ago. Ella reminded them of Aaliyah. Having some small piece of her kept their spirits up.

Parking in my designated spot, I turned the engine off and grabbed my briefcase and white coat. Closing the door on my new BMW SUV, I walked inside, waving to the nurses and cleaning staff. It was pretty quiet for the nine a.m. morning staff.

I was stopped by Daphne, the head nurse. She was one of the only females I considered a friend, as there was nothing sexual between us. She passed me the morning charts of what my day would look like. "You look like shit, Kevin."

"Says the woman wearing two different color shoes," I joked.

She popped me on the shoulder. "Boy, don't hate on my shoes. When was the last time you had a good night's sleep?" She lifted my chin and peered into my eyes.

That was something I wasn't ready to talk about. I'd accepted Aaliyah's death, but sleeping without her beside me at night was still hard. I'd taken a few women to bed to pass the time, but they'd all wanted more from me, something I couldn't give. I got through the days by avoiding the pain at all times. Daphne was like a little sister to me, and her constant checking-in came from a good place.

"Daphne, don't start," I grumbled, walking around her toward my office.

She followed, and I sighed, preparing for another lecture. Opening the door to my office, I turned the light on and hung up my coat. I walked around to my desk, and Daphne sat opposite, narrowing her eyes on me as I dropped into my seat and turned on my computer. Deciding to avoid her stare, I opened my emails and grabbed my pen to make notes.

"Which bimbo did you sleep with now?" Daphne investigated, grabbing the pen out of my hand to stop me from working.

"Aren't your patients calling for you?"

She waved me off. "Don't change the subject. I talked to your mother, and she told me they watched Ella last night because you went out on a date. They sounded excited for you, but I knew what it was."

"What was it, Daphne?"

"Another one-night stand to avoid dealing with your feelings."

"Are you a nurse or a therapist?" I questioned, picking up another pen.

"I'm a nurse, sister, mother, wife, friend, and sometimes, a therapist. Kevin, you need to slow down and talk with someone or at least stop running around with these little bimbos."

"Hey, you're talking about your sister."

"Exactly, and we both know Denise isn't for you, so

please spare me the details. I already have to deal with her attitude when you don't call her back, and she expects me to force you to date her exclusively."

I scrunched my eyes at her statement, shocked her sister would believe I wanted something serious with her. "Denise and I will never be in a relationship. She's too high maintenance."

"I see. Then why did you sleep with her? She works in real estate and thinks the man she marries should have a certain caliber in the community. The girl expects everything to be handed to her," Daphne told me, revealing her sister's secrets.

I knew Denise wanted something more, and I'd repeatedly told her I'd never date or get married again. Hopefully, she'd eventually realize that nothing would make me change my mind. "It's a friendly hookup and nothing else. I don't need to tell her who I was with."

There was a knock at the door. Brianna, the ER nurse I'd had a few nights of passion with, popped her head inside. She looked nervous to see Daphne sitting in my office. I usually didn't fool around with anyone I worked with, but Brianna was persistent. We'd had a few conversations after work and ended up in bed. She'd since become more possessive. She only wanted to be on my floor and made her presence known if I talked with another woman.

"Oh, I didn't notice you weren't alone. I'll come back," Brianna said.

"I was just leaving. Is there something you need, Brianna?" Daphne asked, standing and turning her back to me.

Brianna was a beautiful girl with a slim five-five frame, medium-brown skin tone, and plush lips. Her eyebrows raised at Daphne's question. Usually, the nurses reported to Daphne first in the morning, so there was no reason to be in my office when she should be making her rounds.

"Uh, I was looking for you, Daphne. They told me you were in Kevin's office."

Daphne raised an eyebrow. "You mean Dr. Haven's office?"

Brianna glanced at me and mumbled, "Sorry. Doctor Haven's office."

I sighed, running a hand down my face.

"Well, I'm here, so let's go out to the front station and discuss what's so important that you needed to see me," Daphne said.

Brianna nodded and turned, heading out of my office. Daphne glared at me over her shoulder, and I raised my hands in surrender. I chuckled at her attitude as she closed my door. Daphne reminded me of my little sister, Kelendra, who tried to run my life even though I was eight years older. Kelendra wanted me to get married again so Ella would have a mother to take care of her. She thought I needed a woman to keep me on track.

I pulled my vibrating phone out of my pocket and opened my messages to see a photo of Ella smiling in bed with her teddy bear next to my mom. She wasn't feeling well, and I'd told her it was okay to stay home from kindergarten. I replied to the message with a heart emoji, closed out of my phone, and continued checking my emails and updating my charts.

An hour later, I switched off the computer, grabbed my ER coat, and started my rounds of follow-up visits with patients. My first patient was one of my favorites, Mrs. Louise Little, a seventy-five-year-old woman who'd been in and out of the ER for the past few months after heart surgery.

I knocked on the door and entered her room to find her laughing at something on the TV. "How is my favorite patient doing today?" I always asked about their day before bombarding them with medical questions.

"Hey, Doctor Sexy. I'm doing well. How are you?" Mrs. Little asked, turning the volume down on the latest episode of *Real Housewives*.

She loved calling me Doctor Sexy, and I was used to it at this point, so I let her get away with it. I figured a little flirting kept her spirits up since her husband had died three years ago. She only had her daughter now, who lived out of state and visited when she could.

"I'm doing good, thanks, Mrs. Little. I need to check your vitals. Did you get your breakfast already? I heard French toast was on the menu."

She hung her head in a no. "That crazy girl brought me some damn burnt toast, scrambled eggs, and juice. I want someone else checking on me."

"Why does she have to be crazy?" I knew she was talking about Brianna. Everyone had the same thing to say. She was loud, self-absorbed, and mixed up the patients' meal plans. But she was the Hospital Director's niece, and nepotism went a long way.

"That girl is more concerned with looking good than taking care of us. The next time she tries to force that crap food down my throat, I'm slapping the shit out of her," Mrs. Little barked, shaking her head.

I grinned and lowered her gown a little to check her vitals. "All right. Everything sounds normal. I think I can hook you up with some French toast and tea on the next round of food."

"Thank you, Kevin, but don't send that heathen in here. I heard you had a date last night."

I groaned, knowing Daphne was running her mouth. "It wasn't a date."

"Mmhmm. Tell me everything," Mrs. Little said, then proceeded to turn the volume back up.

I chuckled at her dismissal and updated her vitals on her chart. I left her room and headed for the nurse's station, looking down at my notes. Which is how I collided with someone coming the other way, and we fell in a heap on the floor.

Chapter 2

Kevin

The woman I'd collided with sprawled on top of me, along with the tray of hot food she'd been carrying.

"Shit! Didn't you see me coming?" I growled. My back throbbed, and I'd have to change my clothes.

"It was an accident. I apologize, Doctor," she spat with an attitude.

"Do you realize who I am?" I demanded, snatching the towel out of her hand to clean myself off.

"No, but something tells me you're about to let me know," she responded with the same feisty attitude.

I should ignore her and walk away. Most women found me intimidating, but her scrunched nose, folded arms, and plump lips froze my tongue and made my dick hard. I wanted to put something in her mouth to shut her up, and I could think of just the thing. But I'd promised I wouldn't go there with another nurse after with Brianna.

"Kevin, are you all right?" Daphne ran over with fresh scrubs and helped to clean up the mess.

I took a deep breath. "Yeah. Let me go change." I peered at the woman. "What's your name?"

"Nurse Benson. Nice to meet you, Doctor Haven. I'm assigned to your floor," she stated sarcastically before heading into Mrs. Little's room.

"I want her on another floor," I barked at Daphne as I strode to the bathroom to change.

Daphne followed me into the bathroom. "Stop whining. It was an accident. I'm not moving her to another department."

I grabbed the paper towels from the dispenser, wetted them, and wiped my shirt. Luckily, the food hadn't been scalding hot, or I would've ended up as one of the patients.

I changed my scrubs. "I want her gone," I snapped, ignoring Daphne's glare as I left the bathroom.

"No. She came highly recommended, and I think you should apologize. April is one of the best nurses in the field, and the staff and patients love her. You're just mad she didn't take your shit," Daphne said bluntly, catching me up.

Ducking into my office, I tried to shut and lock my door, but Daphne stuck her foot in the way.

"Stop acting like a baby," she snapped.

"Whatever," I huffed, grabbing another lab coat.

"Brianna is the least efficient nurse on staff, and you haven't raged to get her fired."

"That's because Brianna keeps her mouth shut, even if she is relied upon to do simple tasks."

"Probably doesn't hurt that she keeps your dick in her mouth."

"You're not funny, Daphne."

"I wasn't trying to be. Get over yourself, Kevin, and

get to work. Please be nice to April. I have no plans on her leaving us, and if you do anything to make her want to leave, I'll kick your ass."

"I thought I was your friend."

"Not when it comes to my patients. They love her, and she makes a mean lasagna."

"Did I just hear you correctly? You're placing lasagna over me?"

"Yep. Now run along and be a good doctor." Daphne laughed and patted me on the chest.

I shook my head and left in the opposite direction to Mrs. Little's room, wanting to avoid April at all costs. I wasn't prepared to deal with her again, and if I had my way, she'd be moved by next week.

...

I was on lunch break at Sob's East with Warren four hours later, eating a burger and fries. Warren chuckled as I retold the story of getting food dumped on me earlier.

"I want her transferred to another floor, and Daphne is fighting me." I took a bite of the double cheeseburger and rinsed it down with a bottle of water.

"Is she hot?"

"What does that have to do with anything?" I sighed in annoyance.

"Kevin, you haven't stopped talking about her for the past forty minutes. She's hot and probably won't take your shit like the other women you deal with," Warren observed.

"I didn't look at her long enough. I was too busy trying to get the food off my scrubs."

Warren laughed again, holding up his hand to get

another round of burgers from the waitress at the bar. "What's her name?"

I wiped my mouth with my napkin. "April something."

Warren frowned. "April. Is she about five-six with short hair, hazel eyes, warm brown skin, and a dazzling smile?"

"Yeah. How do you know her?"

"April Benson, the new nurse who transferred here full time a couple of days ago. She visited a few months back, and I met her through Kyla when she took her grandmother for an annual check-up from remission. She's cute and quick to sideline you if you get on her unpleasant side."

"She needs to learn how to walk and talk at the same time."

"I take it you had the pleasure of getting on her nasty side."

I waved him off, leaned back in my chair, and closed my eyes. The buzz of conversation about the latest football game surrounded me. It reminded me of when Aaliyah and I went to the bars and clubs together.

"Get out of your head, man. Aaliyah would want you to move on with your life."

I ran a hand down my face. Warren was right. I needed to stop comparing every woman to Aaliyah. I never brought anyone home. I always met them at hotels or their place. I felt uncomfortable bringing another woman into Ella's world, knowing I would never be serious with them. Kyla, Daphne, my mom, and my sister helped as much as possible with questions I couldn't answer when it came to raising a baby girl.

I grabbed my wallet to split the check as the waitress brought a second burger and fries boxed up in a to-go bag.

"Keep the change," we both said, handing her forty dollars for a twelve-dollar bill.

I stood and scooped up my lab coat and keys to head back to the hospital.

Warren followed behind, heading for his truck parked next to my car. "Kyla wants you to bring Ella over for dinner this weekend."

"I'll check my schedule at the hospital and get back to you tomorrow. Ella stayed out of school today with a fever and cough, so I'm heading to pick her up from my parents after I check on my patients."

Warren nodded. "Sounds good. Keep me updated. And Kevin?"

"Yeah?"

Warren smirked. "Tell April that Warren says hello."

I flipped him off, climbed into my car, and started the ignition. The pub was twenty minutes from the hospital. We'd chosen a place nearby with me being on call. Before driving off, I honked my horn, getting Warren's attention.

"What's up?" he asked.

"How are things at Club Seek?"

He furrowed his brow. "You haven't been in a while."

Not since Aaliyah died. "I know. It all depends on my schedule. I'd hate to get started with something and not be able to take it on fully."

"And you have Ella's school schedule. Being a member is a stress reliever, especially the connection you build with your sub," Warren remarked, backing out of the parking lot and driving off in the opposite direction.

Merging into traffic, I turned the music up and listened to some old-school Luther Vandross. He was one of Aaliyah's favorite singers. Fifteen minutes later, I swiped my badge over the employee entrance security point and parked in my space.

Things were more hectic in the hospital than this morning. Kids sat in the waiting area with their parents, crying. A guy in a wheelchair was filling out paperwork. The local vendor was refilling the vending machine. I stepped behind the nurse's station to see which dire issue I needed to look into before I finished up with the paperwork.

"Anything I'm needed for, Daphne?" I lifted the chart next to her on the incoming patients.

She smacked the file down so I couldn't pick it up. "No. Finish your rounds and head home to my Ella. You've done enough today."

"Daphne, I've given Mrs. Little her dinner for the night, and I'm leaving for the day," April said as she walked up to the station.

I checked my watch. It was a little after three p.m. The first shift didn't leave until five or six.

"Thanks, April. I'll see you tomorrow." Daphne answered, hanging up the phone and grabbing a piece of candy.

April raised her eyes to find me watching her.

"Kind of early for you to leave, don't you think, Mrs. Benson?" I questioned, wanting to push her buttons.

Even in her scrubs, I remembered the melting softness of her body. She was curvy in all the right places, and her full, pouty lips had me wanting to stick something between them.

If only her beauty matched her personality.

Chapter 3

April

It was hard to ignore the authority and confidence Doctor Kevin Haven exuded. It was clear he was made to save lives.

I'd felt the hard muscles that filled out his scrubs first-hand when we collided this morning. At over six feet, with broad shoulders, dark brown skin, and classically handsome features, the man thought he was God's gift to women. I could see how all the women fell so quickly to their knees to please him. But not me. He'd have to do a lot of begging to get in my pants, even if he did have the sexiest lips I'd ever seen.

"*Miss* Benson," I emphasized.

"Well, *Miss* Benson, have you cleared all your patients for the day and filled out your charts?" Doctor Haven demanded.

"I've already cleared everything with Daphne. If you have questions, I think she can answer those for you," I spat, tapping the desk and walking off.

I heard giggles from the other nurses behind me. I

wasn't trying to face off with a doctor my first week here, but he'd exhausted my patience for the day.

The sun was setting, and I needed to get home to finish moving into my apartment. Opening my car door, I dropped my purse on the seat and slipped on my shades. Driving toward the freeway, I headed to my two-bedroom apartment. I was fortunate I'd found it for a reasonable price. Each complex had a pool, a screening room, and a laundry room.

I moved across the country from Las Vegas to start over after I broke off my engagement with my fiancé. Lenny was only interested in having a trophy wife and nothing else. He grew up with the ideal woman on his arm at his beck and call to show off. I grew up needing more out of life and wanting to help people.

After my grandfather died of cancer, I changed my studies from economics to nursing. The love and care the nurses in his hospital gave him made me respect them even more. My parents still lived in Vegas and wanted me happy, whether I was with someone or not. I'd never had to deal with overbearing parents who tried to force me into something I didn't want to do.

Arriving home ten minutes later, I turned the engine off and got out of the car. I lived in a duplex building and was lucky to be on the first floor. As I entered, Big Mamma, my grandfather's cat, was at the door. The cat was ten but got around like the young cats.

I bent to rub her head. "Big Mamma, how are you, girl?"

She pressed up against me, purring the whole time. I picked her up and took her over to the couch with me. The door opened, and my best friend and neighbor came in wearing a housecoat and holding a bag of chips.

Chasity had a spare key I'd given her for emergencies. She sat down beside me, looking miserable.

"What's with the long face?" I asked.

"Ugh, men," Chasity grumbled.

I tittered. "What did Simon do now?"

Chasity laid her head on my shoulder, and Big Mamma crawled onto her lap. "He canceled our dinner plans tonight because of work. I'm pissed because I wanted to wear the new dress I bought for our one-year anniversary."

"Chasity, you knew he had an important job from the beginning. He didn't hide the security work he does for Warren and Morris. Give him a break," I advised, standing and heading to my bedroom to shower and change.

Chasity followed behind me, moping. "I know. I try not to bring it up, but he works a lot, and we barely have time together."

I grabbed fresh underwear and my robe and headed to the bathroom. "Simon loves you, Chasity. The man worships the ground you walk on. Don't look for problems," I called from the bathroom and closed the door.

I turned on the water, set it to the perfect temperature, and pulled my hair into my bonnet to avoid getting it wet. Taking off my top and pants, I dumped them in the hamper and stepped under the water. Picking up my strawberry body wash, I rinsed the day away.

Twenty minutes later, I merged from the bedroom in my robe. Chasity was draped across my bed, watching TV with her lip poked out. "Find something to wear and meet me by the car in fifteen minutes. I'm taking you out," I instructed.

"I'm not in the mood, April."

"You need this, and I need a drink. I'm calling Kyla. You go call someone, and we'll make it girl's night out."

"That does sound good. Okay, I'll change and call my cousin to meet us at the bar." Chasity jumped up and left to go upstairs to her apartment.

Looking through my closet, I ran my hand over my dresses and grabbed a low-cut, short sweater dress and black boots. Removing my bonnet, I shook my hair out and changed into my dress. I applied clear lip gloss and mascara and found my black clutch.

Wandering to the kitchen, I replaced the water and cat food for Big Mamma. I grabbed my jacket and stepped outside. Chasity came downstairs as I opened the door of my new Honda Accord I'd bought when I moved. I took my phone out of my purse and dialed Kyla's number.

"Hello."

I bit back a grin. "Kyla!"

"Hey, April. How are you doing?" Kyla asked.

"I'm good, honey. Get dressed and tell Warren and the boys you'll hang out with your girls tonight."

"I heard that!" Warren yelled over the phone.

Kyla laughed at his outburst. "Do you mind if I go out for a little while?" I heard Kyla ask him. I heard shuffling on the other end, and she came back on the call. "Text me the address of where you want to meet."

"Sounds good, babe. Text you in a second." I ended the call and texted the address to Kyla.

"Do they still practice the Dom and Sub lifestyle?" Chasity questioned.

I reversed out of my parking space and drove off toward Flight Bar and Grill. "You know I can't talk about that. It's private. Are you interested in a Dom and Sub lifestyle with Simon?" I inquired.

Chasity shrugged. "Simon wants to take me to the club to see if I'd be interested in joining. I don't know if I want to put myself out there like that, though."

I nodded in understanding as I turned into the parking lot of Flight Bar and Grill. I'd heard it was a bar where single women hung out in hopes of finding a guy to help relieve some stress. I hadn't had sex for six months, and the men I'd met here so far hadn't sparked my desire to sleep with them.

Checking my hair and makeup, we stepped out of the car, and I followed Chasity inside. She glanced around the room and waved at a woman wearing a long red off-the-shoulder dress. Chasity grabbed my hand and led me over to the table, greeting the woman with a hug.

"April, this is my cousin, Denise. Denise, this is my best friend I talk about all the time," Chasity said, gesturing toward me.

I extended my hand for a shake, but Denise ignored it and gave me a fake smile.

"Rude," I mumbled.

"Chasity, you look cute. Did Simon buy your dress?" Denise asked, turning to her cousin.

Chasity shook her head. "No. I bought this with my money, girl."

"There's nothing like spending your man's money on yourself," Denise declared, holding up her hand for a high five.

Chasity returned it. I could already tell what kind of night this would be.

A tap on my shoulder made me turn to see Kyla sitting next to me. "Thank God you came," I sighed.

The server came over to our table and passed menus around. She placed a glass of water and straws out for everyone. "Hi, ladies. I'm Abigail. I'll be your server tonight. What would you like to drink?"

"Kyla, this is my cousin, Denise." Chasity introduced once we'd placed our orders.

Kyla held out her hand toward Denise, and she accepted the gesture. I didn't know if I should be pissed off or grateful.

"Nice to meet you, Denise. Do you work at the hospital too?" Kyla asked.

Denise shook her head no. "Oh, no, girl. I wouldn't be caught dead around sick people. Gives me the creeps."

"Um, Denise, that's offensive," I responded.

"Excuse me?" Denise retorted.

"It's fine, April," Kyla commented, waving off Denise's statement.

"I suggest you rethink your words. You should be grateful for nurses and doctors because the second you get sick, you'll call on them to take care of you. Kyla is a cancer survivor. Does she look sick to you?" I raised an eyebrow.

"Chasity, who is this girl again?" Denise demanded.

I shot her a dirty look. "*This girl* is April. Direct your attitude over here, sweetie."

Chasity leaned forward on the table. "Ladies, please. We want to have a fun evening. Let's all calm down."

Denise flipped her hair and opened her mouth to say something when her eyes widened, and she screeched loudly. She jumped out of her seat and threw her arms around the last person I expected to see tonight.

Dr. Kevin Haven was here with Kyla's husband, Warren.

Chapter 4

Kevin

Warren called me an hour ago, wanting to see what Kyla was up to on a girl's night out. Brianna was pissing me off with constantly texting and calling. I figured my parents wouldn't mind watching Ella for the night, so I went home, showered, and changed.

I removed Denise's arms from around my neck and stepped out of her reach. She always tried to make it seem like we had a relationship when it was just casual sex.

"Babe, I'm happy to see you. I missed you today," Denise confessed, grasping my hand. She tried to kiss me on the lips, but I turned my head, and her kiss landed on my cheek.

April gave us a harsh glare. Seeing her here was a shock.

Yanking my hand back, I sat between Warren and Denise.

Kyla kissed Warren. "Who's watching the boys?'

"Kristen and Devon," Warren replied, wrapping his arm around her shoulders and pulling her close.

"You can't speak?" I questioned, staring directly at April.

"I speak to the people I want to speak to, Doctor Haven," April stated bluntly.

I grinned, loving how my mere presence pissed her off. "At least you haven't tossed food all over me," I responded sarcastically.

Denise looked between April and me. "Do you know each other?"

"No!" April and I said in unison.

"April, I heard you made a big impression on Kevin today," Warren teased.

The server appeared with menus and took everyone's orders.

"I'll have the beer, barbeque ribs, and fries on the side," I said, passing Denise my menu.

"What about sharing a salad, baby? Barbeque is fattening," she remarked.

"Get that if you want. I'm having barbeque and fries."

Denise ordered a red wine, and the server took the rest of our food orders.

"*If* you have something to say, Ashley, please enlighten the group," Denise said, glaring across the table at April, who was trying to conceal a smile.

Chasity covered her face with her hand and groaned in embarrassment. I liked Chasity. She was laid back—the complete opposite of her cousin. Chasity and I met through Denise at the hospital holiday party at Sob's Pub a few months back.

"First, you know my name is April. Second, if you were any closer to that man, you'd be his shadow. If you weren't so oblivious—"

Chasity cut April off by covering her mouth with a napkin.

"Whatever," Denise muttered.

The atmosphere was tense. I wanted to chill tonight, but the two women were clearly having a pissing contest.

"Warren, how is work at the security firm and your properties?" April asked, breaking the silence.

"Business is doing good, April. You should check out some properties when you're ready to move into a house," Warren replied.

April brushed a piece of hair behind her ear. "I'll keep that in mind. I want to start a foundation for when I'm ready to have kids. But first, I need a relationship like you and Kyla." April smiled, pointing between them.

The server brought the food out for everybody. Kyla had ordered a salad. April and Chasity had ordered burgers and fries. Denise tried to take a French fry off my plate, and I pulled it away.

"Babe, you have to share," she whined.

"Denise, stop calling me babe. It's Kevin," I reminded her as I reached for the ketchup at the same time as April. I backed off to let her go first.

"You tease too much, Kevin." Denise giggled and slapped my shoulder.

I waved off her words like they were mosquitoes.

"So, I was thinking we could go to the beach this weekend," she said, grasping my hand.

A pained look marred April's face. I wasn't sure if it was because Denise was nuzzling up against me or giving out details of a potential date, which I don't do. I didn't know why she was trying so hard to make it look like we were in a relationship.

My brow furrowed. "I have plans this weekend, and you know I don't date, Denise."

The server returned before Denise could reply. "Is everybody doing okay? Anyone need any more food or drinks?"

All the girls shook their heads no, along with Warren.

"Can I get the check and a to-go box?" April asked.

"Sure, one check or splitting?" the server questioned.

"Split," April replied.

"One check," I said at the same time. "It's on me. A welcome to Baptist Memorial Hospital."

A frown crossed her face. "I can pay for myself." She reached in her purse for her wallet.

"Are you going to challenge me on a ten-dollar bill?" I fussed, snatching the bill from the server.

April leaned over and grabbed it out of my hand. "Yep," she said, removing her money from her wallet.

I groaned, rubbing my chin to calm myself down.

"Why are you being a bitch? He's offering to pay," Denise snapped.

"Denise, apologize to April. That was uncalled for," Chasity said, trying to defuse the situation.

"No, she meant that, Chasity. I *was* being nice, but if you want to see the bitch, I can bring her out." April drummed her fingers on the table.

"How about I take care of the bill, and everyone leaves with a smile?" Warren insisted, taking the ticket from April.

He removed his credit card and handed it off to the server. I pulled some bills from my wallet and tipped fifty dollars. April stood and left, with Chasity following behind. I started to stand, wanting to know what her problem was, but Denise blocked me from leaving.

"Are you sleeping with her, Kevin?" Denise jabbed her finger into my chest.

"No," I grunted.

"All right, that's our cue to leave, honey," Warren stated, helping Kyla out of her seat.

She kissed me on the cheek as I shook hands with Warren and told him I'd talk with him tomorrow.

"I don't believe you," Denise snapped.

"Okay." I turned to leave.

Denise grabbed my arm. "Why does she hate you so much if you're not sleeping with her?"

I shrugged, not feeling the need to explain myself. It was none of Denise's business. I'd never sleep with someone like April, but she didn't need to know that.

I peeled her hand off my arm. "I need to get home for an early shift tomorrow."

"Can I come over?" she begged.

"Denise, you know I only call you when I'm in the mood, and right now, I'm not. I'll talk to you later."

As I left, I noticed Chasity and April driving off. I shook my head in annoyance. That woman was more trouble than she was worth.

Chapter 5

April

I hadn't seen Doctor Evil for a week, and my days were going well with my patients. Daphne allowed me to pick up more hours whenever she had a call out, or someone was running late. This hospital ran much smoother than my previous one, and I was grateful for the promotion opportunities.

"How is old man Jacobs in room three fifty, April?" Daphne asked as I updated medicine for the floor before I made the rounds.

"He's grumpy as usual. Only wants you to check up on him."

Daphne laughed and grabbed a pair of gloves off the medical cart next to me.

"Daphne!" Denise marched over, wearing a red catsuit that showed off her cleavage.

"Denise, what are you doing here?" Daphne questioned.

"I have a lunch date with my man," she said smugly.

"You'll have to wait. He's checking on Mrs. Little right now," Daphne told her.

"That's fine." Denise scrunched up her nose. "When are you going to stop working at this place?"

"You mean the hospital? A place where people get better? A place you may need one day?" I asked harshly.

"No offense, but she can do better than this place," Denise responded, lowering her shades and peering at me.

"Do you two know each other?" Daphne gestured between us.

"No!" we said at the same time.

Kevin walked out of Mrs. Little's room as I turned to step inside, and we almost collided again. His hands went to my waist to steady me, and I froze.

"Sorry," he said, removing his hands as if he'd been burned.

My eyes darted from his hands to his lips. "Yeah. Can I get by?"

"Oh, sure... Sorry," he muttered and stepped aside.

As I closed the door, I heard Denise say, "Baby, I'm ready for lunch."

I gritted my teeth. Her voice was like nails on a chalkboard.

...

"Hey, Mrs. Little. I have your medicine." I poured a glass of water and passed her the prescription pills.

She sat up and took the water and pills. "I hate being in the hospital."

"I know, but the doctor said you're responding to the medicine, and your heart isn't giving you any trouble. Hopefully, you can go home soon."

"I never thought I would make it those first few

months after my Leon passed away, let alone two years. Now, I might be reunited with him."

"Don't talk like that, Mrs. Little."

"Honey, I'm an old woman. I know tomorrow is not promised, but it's nice to know I'll have someone waiting on me when I go."

"Well, that time is not now. So, what are you watching on TV?"

"That damn *Real Housewives* show. Those folks are too rich to be that dumb," she joked.

I smiled and pulled up a chair to watch the episode with her.

Hours later, I let myself into my apartment as Chasity came down the stairs and headed toward me. I smiled. "Right on time for a wine and chocolate night."

"I can go for that." Chasity frowned, following me inside.

"Why do you look so down?" I questioned.

"I'm pissed because Simon has to work at Club Seek tonight."

"You knew his job involved that kind of security, and Club Seek is renowned in his business realm," I said.

"Yeah, but an underground BDSM club?" Chasity exhaled a weary breath.

Shutting the front door behind her, I placed my keys and purse on the couch. "He's a professional. Never took you for the jealous type."

Chasity flopped down on the recliner. "I'm not, but he works with so many single women, and it's exclusive, so you have to get checked out before going."

"Well, I think Kyla's husband is friends with the owners."

Chasity perked up. "You think she could get us inside?"

"I don't know, Chasity. It's pretty last minute."

"I know, but we haven't had any alone time, and I miss my man. Who knows what he's surrounded by in the club."

"You trust Simon, don't you? Otherwise, there's no use in being in a relationship."

"I trust him, but I don't look like those girls."

I waved her off. "You look fine."

"Can you see if Kyla would take us?" Chasity begged.

"Let me call her." Kicking my shoes off and jacket on the sofa, I pulled my phone out of my pocket and dialed Kyla's number. The phone rang for a minute until I heard kids playing in the background.

"Warren Jr., stop throwing water balloons at your brother," Kyla yelled, and I heard laughing through the phone.

I admired how she'd transitioned from a celebrity actress to a mom.

"Hey, April."

"Kyla, I need a favor, and I'm hoping you won't say no."

"Is it life or death?" she deadpanned.

I chuckled. "Depends on the outcome."

"What's the favor?"

"Chasity wants to go to Club Seek tonight."

Chapter 6

April

"**Y**ou have to go through extensive background checks to get inside as guests," Kyla informed me.

"I know, but she wants to see Simon, and I'd appreciate you submitting us as guests for the night. I've never been to one of these places."

"Are you a submissive?" Kyla investigated.

"Oh, God, no! I would probably end up in jail with the things I've heard," I joked.

"There are some awful examples of being in a submissive and dominant relationship, but for the most part, it's a beautiful thing," Kyla told me.

"I know you're a member of the lifestyle."

"A long-time member. You'd run for the hills if you got with someone who didn't understand your boundaries and concerns ahead of time."

Nodding, I closed my eyes, thinking over her words. I thought about my ex-fiancé wanting me to get married, have kids, and conform to his lifestyle. Something I knew would end in a divorce within a year. Glad I got out of that relationship. "You're probably right. But this is about Chasity tonight."

"Let me call you back after I talk with Warren," Kyla said.

"Okay." I ended the call, seeing Chasity's defeated expression. "I still have the wine and chocolate."

* * *

Forty-five minutes later, Warren and Kyla escorted us inside Club Seek. I'd contacted Kyla about getting into the club so Chasity could see Simon, but I couldn't help but be curious.

I wore a red one-shoulder halter top that exposed my belly button and piercing. The skirt was black with a side split, and my hair was up, showing off my neckline. Chasity was more conservative than me. I guess she figured surprising Simon dressed too provocatively while he was working wouldn't be a good idea.

"This place is huge," Chasity said.

We passed through a lobby and into the bar area on the second floor, where we were given red wristbands.

"They have over two hundred masters and security at all times," Warren explained." Simon often works the night shift to ensure the submissives are safe. There are multiple theme rooms. All play scenes are below in the lounge area."

"What's a master?" Chasity asked.

"A dom is a man on top of things in a scene. More of a sexual dominant in the bedroom," Kyla informed her.

"Let's check out a scene in the pit." Warren escorted us down the grand staircase below.

"I've heard about this type of club. Never seen one in

person," Chasity admitted, her eyes widening at the naked woman tied to a bench with her legs spread.

"What are that woman and man doing?" I questioned. He was wearing a mask and was running a feather-like item down her stomach. Her hands and feet were tied to the bench so she couldn't move.

"He's pleasuring her with a feather and covering her eyes with a scarf. It's called sensation play," Warren informed me.

"Damn," I mumbled as she moaned.

"Every scene is different. Some like feather play. Others like spanking. There are lots of different toys. But we ensure all submissives are comfortable with any scene they consent to," Warren remarked.

"Who's that guy?" I asked.

Right as the girl moaned through an orgasm, the guy removed his mask. My mouth dropped to the floor. It was Doctor Haven.

"Oh, my God!" I shouted.

Everyone looked at me, including Kevin. The look on his face told me I'd be in trouble if I spoke of this to anyone.

"You signed a confidentiality agreement, April," Warren reminded me.

I nodded that I understood. Trying not to look at Doctor Haven without a shirt was hard. The man was sculpted like a god. He released his Sub and helped her up, and they left the room.

Minutes later, Kevin marched toward me, still shirt-less. He gripped my arm and pulled me off to the side. "What the hell are you doing here?"

His scent filled my nostrils, and I hated my reaction to

his proximity. "I could ask you the same question, Doctor Haven."

"Don't get smart with me, April."

"Is everything all right?" Warren asked, clasping Kevin's shoulder.

I tore my gaze from Kevin to look at Warren. "We're fine, Warren. I was just surprised to see Doctor Haven here."

"Kevin is one of our members. He's a Dom," Warren replied.

Kevin didn't remove his eyes from me. "Warren, why is she here?"

"Warren's not my father. I can speak for myself," I spat, yanking my arm out of his grip.

Kevin released a long breath. "You shouldn't be here."

Was he seriously trying to be the boss of me? "Why not? You're here."

"Warren, why is she here?" Kevin demanded, his tone stern.

"Warren doesn't speak for me," I repeated, moving around him and taking Chasity's arm to leave.

An arm wrapped around my waist from behind and lifted me.

"Put me down!" I hissed.

Warren stood watching, his mouth twitching with a smile.

"Warren, I'll call you tomorrow," Kevin said, heading for the door.

"Kyla! Help me."

Kevin slapped my ass, pushed the door open, and walked to his car. He opened the passenger side and set me on my feet. I tried to get out of his arms, and he pressed his body against me, pinning me against the car. His thick arousal dug into my stomach.

"You're not wearing a shirt," I whispered.

Kevin shook his head. "You have no business being here."

I lifted my chin. "You're not my man. I can do whatever I want."

"You should be happy I'm not your man. I'd spank you right now."

"Doctor Haven," I groaned.

"Get in the car, April," he demanded.

I got inside, moving my skirt so it wouldn't get trapped in the door. I caught his gaze on my thighs and rolled my eyes. "Asshole," I mumbled.

He came around to the driver's side, got in, and buckled his seatbelt. "Where am I taking you?" he asked, starting the car.

"2200 Jasper Road." I turned the music on to avoid talking to him.

He smacked my hand away. "Don't touch my radio."

"Are you an asshole with me or with everyone?" I snapped.

"I only give back what I get, and that mouth of yours is trouble."

I spied the child seat in the back. "Are you this grumpy with your daughter?"

"Who told you about my daughter?"

"Daphne and then Chasity after our first encounter."

"Ella sees the best of me," he commented, pulling up to my house.

"Thanks for the ride," I said, reaching for the door.

He gripped my arm, stopping me from leaving. "A lady never opens her own door when she's with me."

"Sorry." I removed my hand, waiting for him to come around to my side of the door.

Kevin held his hand out to help me out of the car.

"Thanks. You don't have to walk me to the door."

"Do you ever tire of this?" He motioned a hand up and down me.

"Tire of what?" I said, crossing my arms over my chest.

"This! We got off on the wrong foot, and I'm sorry I overreacted. But you're as much at fault with your attitude. Calm the fuck down, and let me walk you to the door."

"Does Denise let you talk to her like this? Because I think you've mistaken me for her," I said as we reached my front door.

Chapter 7

April

Warren's car pulled up, and Chasity emerged from the backseat.

"Denise is not my woman," Kevin said, following me inside my apartment.

"Could have fooled me. Anyway, thank you for the ride. I'm home safe now, and I'll hit up the club another day when you're not there. Maybe we should cross-reference our calendars," I joked, sitting on my loveseat and crossing my legs.

Chasity marched in and pushed him in the chest. It was comical because he didn't move an inch. "Simon is pissed now, and he won't even talk to me," she whined.

Warren led Kyla to the couch, and Chasity came to sit next to me.

"Stay out of the club, April. It's not for you." Kevin stood in front of me.

"Not for me? Is that a challenge, Doctor?"

"You two should cool off," Warren stated.

"This reminds me of the time your brother came to

35

the club and tried to proposition me, Warren. It didn't end well, and you were suspended from playing for twelve weeks," Kyla explained.

"Wow, the place sounds strict," I said.

"For good reason. I trust everyone in there, and if you got involved, you'd be taken care of," Kyla told me.

"She's not joining," Kevin said, sliding his hands into his pants pockets.

All glanced around the room. All eyes were on me for a rebuttal, but I wouldn't play his games. "Kyla, I think I'll look into the club. I enjoy trying new things."

"We need to get going, baby. The kids will be wondering when we're coming home," Warren muttered.

He tapped Kyla on the thigh, and she hugged Kevin, Chasity, and me while Warren shook hands with Kevin.

"I'm going to call Simon. Maybe he'll try that feather trick on me after his shift," Chasity informed us, leaving Kevin and me alone.

The tension stretched between us.

"I need to get going," Kevin said.

"Tell Ella I said hello," I mumbled, but he'd already closed the door.

I sighed in frustration, exhausted after a long day at work and dealing with an angry Dom. Still, a forbidden thought whispered through my mind.

Could I be a submissive for Kevin?

...

The next morning, I stepped into the elevator to see Kevin standing in the corner with his head down.

"Morning," I muttered, trying to be the bigger person

and not cause any friction. Too often, we'd gotten into a heated argument, and I wasn't going to continue down that path.

"Morning," he replied in his deep raspy voice.

The elevator filled up a few minutes later, causing me to be pushed into the corner with my back to his chest. His warm breath stirred the hairs on my neck, and my stomach fluttered. As the elevator continued to rise, it jumped and stalled.

"Oh shit!" I yelped.

A strong hand wrapped around my waist, pulling me against him. "Relax. I've got you," he whispered, his hands spreading over my stomach.

I nodded, trying to calm my nerves.

"This elevator is always acting up. It should get going in a minute," another nurse said.

The lights were out, and I tensed, taking deep breaths.

"Are you claustrophobic?" Kevin murmured.

"No, but it's getting hot in here." I fanned myself.

Ten minutes turned into forty and then two hours.

"Don't make a sound," I heard in my ear as a hand slid under my shirt.

I gasped in shock as he cupped my breast and pushed my hair to the side, kissing behind my ear. He pulled the bra cup down and flicked my nipple between his thumb and index finger. I gripped his thigh, melting under his touch.

"Open your eyes," he whispered.

I shook my head no. "Someone will see."

"Let them. I like it when they watch." He slid my panties to the side and rubbed his thumb against my folds.

"Kevin," I moaned out, opening my legs.

"Open your eyes."

I opened my eyes and noticed we were alone in the elevator.

"Come for me, April."

"No."

"April? The elevator started back up."

"What did you say?" I jerked out of Kevin's hold. Everyone was looking at me like I was crazy."

Kevin frowned. "Are you okay?"

"Did you... Wait..." I skimmed my hands over my body to find my clothes intact. Had I imagined it? Fallen asleep?

"Maybe you should let me check you out," Kevin suggested as we exited the elevator and walked down the hall. "You look a little flushed."

I shook my head. "I could have sworn we were..."

"We were what?" Kevin peered down at me.

I was about to answer when Brianna came over and stood between us. "Hey, babe. I have these forms for you to sign off on," she said, popping her bubble gum.

"Brianna, we're in a professional setting, and I'm not your boyfriend," Kevin reminded her as he continued walking.

"Stop being silly, Kevin," Brianna cackled, bumping his shoulder with hers.

"I've been looking all over for you two," Daphne remarked as we approached the nurse's station.

"We got stuck in the elevator," I responded.

"April, we have a meeting. You too, Brianna. Leave Doctor Haven alone," Daphne fussed, pulling Brianna away from Kevin.

"Okay. Let me put my stuff in my locker, and I'll meet

you in the staff room." I glanced over my shoulder as I walked away and caught Kevin staring at my ass. I smiled. *Am I smiling at his response to my body?*

My smile dropped. I couldn't get caught up in another man.

Chapter 8

Kevin

One month later

Things at the hospital seemed to calm down with April. We got along a lot better—so much better that she and I had decided to have dinner tonight. An official date—something I thought I would never go on with another woman. Brianna and Denise could only say they'd had my dick and nothing else.

"Daddy, can I have a new dress?" Ella asked.

I was driving Ella to the park for a few hours. She spent a lot of time with my parents, sister, and Daphne, so it was good to have some daddy-and-daughter time.

"Little nugget, didn't I just buy you new clothes?"

"Warren Jr. and Kylan have extra clothes for school, and I don't want to be left out."

"If you're good today, we'll see."

"Is Uncle Warren bringing Warren Jr and Kylan to the park?" Ella questioned.

"Yes, and I have your snacks, so you won't get hungry, baby," I said, turning into the park.

"Yay!" Ella cheered, clapping her hands. She looked more and more like Aaliyah every day.

"Remember, you have to be a good girl and eat all your snacks, and we'll go to the mall later in the week," I bribed, doing the only thing I knew would work on her to keep her in check. I spoiled my baby rotten and had no one to blame anyone but myself and my parents.

Grabbing the bag of food and a blanket, I picked up Ella and walked toward the bench where Warren, Kyla, and the kids sat waiting, along with another guest I hadn't expected to see.

I set Ella down, and she ran off to the slide with Warren Jr. and Kylan.

"Warren, Kyla, good to see you," I greeted before turning to April. "I'm surprised you're here."

"Kyla told me we were going to the mall. I didn't realize we were coming via the park," April replied.

"I had to do the same thing with Ella. She wants new clothes, so I bribed her with the park and a picnic. My baby's spoiled," I admitted.

"She's beautiful," April said.

"Thanks. She takes after her mother," I answered.

April fidgeted with her hands. "Kyla told me about Aaliyah. I'm sorry for your loss, Kevin."

I raised an eyebrow. "I like this April," I joked, poking her in the side.

She slapped my hand away and laughed.

"I heard you two are going out on a date," Kyla teased, winking at April.

"Only dinner," April said quickly.

"I wanted to apologize properly after our many... disagreements," I added.

"You don't have to do that," April said.

"I want to," I answered, biting into an apple.

Ella ran over, out of breath. "Daddy, I need water." She squeezed between my legs, hiding her face.

"Ella, I want you to meet someone. This is my friend, April Benson." I turned her around.

April smiled. "Hi, Ella, I'm April. I've heard a lot about you, and everything was true."

Ella placed a hand on her hip and tilted her head. "What did you hear?"

"Nugget, what are you doing? Who taught you to stand like that?" I questioned.

April, Kyla, and Warren laughed at her posing. Their reaction threw me off because I'd never seen her act this way.

April giggled. "All good things, baby girl. You're beautiful, just like your mom."

"You knew my mommy?" Ella asked.

April shook her head no. "I saw a picture of her, and you have her eyes and beautiful smile."

"What do you say, Ella?" I rubbed her back, and she grinned at April.

"Thank you, Mrs. Benson," Ella said, wiping the sweat off her face.

"Call me April, sweetie," April said, passing her bottled water.

She ran back off to the field to play with the other kids.

"She's going to be a handful when she gets older." April laughed.

I agreed, running a hand across the back of my neck. We continued watching the kids play and talked about our days at the hospital and everyday parenting.

...

That same night, I showered and changed, then cooked a light meal of sushi and orange glazed chicken and rice. Lighting the candles, I checked on Ella again before closing her bedroom door.

I'd offered to pick April up, but she'd declined, so I gave her the address and asked her to arrive around eight-thirty. Usually, Ella went to bed around nine, but she was tired after playing in the park. I gave her a bath and dinner, and she was asleep before the end of her bedtime story.

The doorbell rang, and I ran down the stairs to open the door. April was dressed in a black sheer dress and had her hair pulled into a ponytail with curls framing her face.

"Hi."

"Wow, you look amazing."

"Is that a good or bad thing?" She chuckled.

"Best thing." I stepped aside to let her in and gestured to the sofa. "Did you have trouble finding my place?" I asked, closing the door.

"No, you're not that far from me."

"That's true. Would you like something to drink? I have wine, water, tea."

"This is a date, right?"

"Why do you ask?"

"Because you're offering me tea on a date. Usually, it's wine or some fancy drink for a first date."

I smirked. "So, you're planning on more dates?"

She placed her purse on the table and crossed her legs. "Depends."

"On what?"

"A few things. How this date goes. If you're an excellent kisser." She quirked an eyebrow. "If you have your other girlfriends in check."

I walked toward the kitchen and grabbed the champagne from the fridge. The living room and dining room were next to each other, and the kitchen was off to the side with a door leading to the garage.

I handed April a glass of champagne. "Here. To answer your concerns, I don't have any girlfriends, and I'm a good cook and kisser for top and bottom."

"What's top and bottom?" she asked, sipping the sparkling champagne.

"Your top lips and bottom pussy lips."

She choked on her champagne. "Warn a girl before you start talking nasty, Doctor."

I gently slapped her back to help her out. "We're both grownups, April. I think we've established we don't like games, and whatever this is needs to be explored. But as you witnessed, I have particular needs. I know you're not familiar with that world."

"Teach me."

"Do you have questions or concerns?"

"I'm not calling you master, and I'm not down with the beatings."

"That's not my kink either. I want to please my sub, fulfill her every desire while I receive pleasure from looking into her eyes and knowing she's at the point of no return," I explained.

"Do you explore the Dom and Sub lifestyle out of the club?"

"I don't because of the women I've been with. I wouldn't pressure anyone into anything they're not comfortable with."

April nodded. "What did you cook?" she asked, changing the subject.

"I hope you like sushi, orange chicken, and rice. Aaliyah was the better cook between us, but I can do a few things. Sorry. I keep bringing her up."

"It's fine, Kevin. I understand. I was engaged once. He wanted me to be the dutiful and meek wife. You've met me. Do I seem like the quiet do-as-you're-told type?" April asked playfully, tilting her head and cupping her cheek.

I grinned. "That's a trick question, and I'm not falling for it. Let's go to the dining room and continue this conversation."

"It smells good, and I'm starving. Tell me about your little girlfriends," she said as I held the chair out for her to take a seat.

I placed her napkin on her lap and poured more champagne into our glasses. "Again, I don't have a girlfriend. I won't lie; I love sex and have needs. Denise and Brianna have been available to take care of those needs. But it's nothing serious."

"So why am I here?" April questioned.

"You're different."

"In what way?" I picked up the fork, popped a piece of chicken in my mouth, and swallowed it down with the champagne. "Fire."

"What?" She looked perplexed by my comment.

"The second you talked back to me, I felt a fire deep in my gut. I can't explain my attraction beyond the obvious. You're gorgeous, confident, smart, and a spitfire. Plus, I like that you don't let me walk all over you."

"I like you too."

"Are you interested in learning about the Dom and Sub lifestyle?"

"I am. I have to confess, the day they locked us in the elevator, I had a little daydream about you. It played into what I saw at Club Seek."

"What was that?"

"You directed my pleasure and commanded it in a voice that I felt comfortable in your arms to let go and be free. Weird, honestly, and I truly am interested in knowing what it's like."

"I'd love to show you. You'll need a safe word, so think of something for when we have our first session."

"Okay. My only restrictions are beatings. I don't mind a little smack on the ass, but from what I've read, some people like the sadist type of play, and that's not me," April said, narrowing her eyes at me.

I held a hand up in surrender. "Baby, you don't have to worry about that with me," I said with a chuckle, lifting the avocado roll into her mouth.

We continued talking and getting to know each other for the rest of the night and made plans to have our first session.

Chapter 9

Kevin

A week later, I'd dealt with everything in order to move forward with April. However, Brianna and Denise kept blowing my phone up. Just like I knew they would.

Denise stood in front of me, preventing me from getting into my car. She was making my decision to block her from my life easy, and that was sad. She was a gorgeous woman, but we'd agreed from the start that our arrangement was only for fun.

"Kevin, you promised you'd call me. I miss you, baby," Denise said, reaching her arms around my neck and trying to kiss me on the lips.

I dodged her lips, and she kissed my cheek. I gently pushed her back. "Denise, you knew the score when you agreed to our arrangement. This was fun, and we have mutual respect, but I never promised anything long-term."

"Who is she? I know there's someone else!"

Shaking my head no, I tried to move around her again.

She placed one hand on her hip and the other on my chest, blocking me.

"Kevin!" I heard my name and looked over my shoulder.

"Who is that bitch?" Denise screamed.

"I'm his woman, and you need to get your hands off him," Brianna spat, grasping my arm and pushing me aside.

Brianna and Denise argued back and forth, causing a scene.

"Ladies, please calm down. You're embarrassing yourselves and me," I groaned, pulling them away from each other. I motioned for the security guard to help me keep them apart.

"That's funny because I've been by his side every day unless I had to work," Denise lied.

"Stop lying, Denise. And Brianna, go back inside," I told them, trying to get things under control.

A car pulled up and parked. April and Chasity got out, shaking their heads.

"Great. Here's another one of your slut buckets," Denise snapped, pushing April's buttons.

Her insult reflected more on her than April, especially since April and I hadn't connected on that level yet. Since I'd met her, I hadn't seen her with anyone else.

April laughed at Denise's comment. "Sweetie, I'm not seeing your boyfriend. You should be worried about Brianna and less about me," April chastised, heading inside.

"Brianna. Leave now," I instructed.

"This isn't over, Kevin," Brianna huffed, storming off to the front entrance of the hospital.

"Denise, I'm not dealing with you anymore. I made it

clear that I'm not interested in you any longer. Move on and find someone who can offer what you want," I said, trying not to deflate her ego.

She teared up and grabbed my arm. "I love you. Kevin."

I shook my head. "I'm sorry, but I don't feel the same."

I kissed her on the forehead and got in my car. I drove off and ended up at the pub. Warren came to meet me and listened to me rant about my day.

"Chasity and April texted Kyla about your little lover's fight," Warren joked as the bartender brought me another shot of scotch.

"Man, that's the last thing I need right now."

"That happens when you're juggling multiple women. I was glad when Kyla walked into my life. I never looked back," Warren remarked, taking a sip of his drink.

"I like April," I mumbled under my breath.

"No, really?" Warren said sarcastically.

"She pisses me off and challenges everything I say, but all I want to do is kiss her." I pulled a twenty from my wallet and placed it in the tip jar. "Is it so wrong to have feelings for her? April reminds me of Aaliyah, and I might have blown it after our first date."

"Be honest with her, and she'll understand. What does Ella think of her?"

"Ella already loves her, and she only spent a short amount of time with her in the park. That makes me feel good. I need to pick her up from my parents in an hour. We have movie night every Friday, and she gets to choose."

"Don't force it. Take your time. You don't want to end up like Kyla and me. We let fear keep us apart for so long."

"Are you going to Club Seek tonight?" I asked.

Warren picked up his drink. "Yeah"

"Thanks for introducing me to the club. It helps me to relax."

"No problem. Don't create another situation like the last time, or you'll get kicked out for making a scene."

I watched as he grabbed his vibrating phone out of his pocket. A smirk appeared across his face.

"Get out of here and go see your woman," I said.

I pulled up at my parents' house one hour later and cut the engine. I got out, grabbed the bouquet of flowers, and knocked on the door. My father yelled that the door was open, and I walked inside.

"What's going on, son? You trying to outdo me with my wife, buying her flowers and shit?" He laughed, pretending to box and throw a fist to my stomach.

I chuckled and blocked the shot, kissing my mother on the cheek and passing her the flowers.

"These are beautiful, Kevin. What did I do to deserve flowers?" my mother asked as she went to get a vase.

"For just being the best mother in the world and helping me with Ella. Where is she?"

"I'm right here, Daddy!" Ella shouted, running from the back room into my arms.

I picked her up and kissed her all over her face. She giggled, trying to block my lips with her hands.

"Hey, nugget."

"Did you bring me something?" Ella asked.

"I have to bring you something to get some love?"

"Duh!" she said, throwing her hands up dramatically.

My dad and I laughed at her antics. I let her down, and she ran off to her play area with the mat and toys my parents had set up for her. That damn *Frozen* movie was on the TV again.

"You staying for dinner, son?" Mom asked.

"Sure. I don't have any plans besides watching a movie with Ella."

"I'll set a place for you."

"Eve, stop babying the man," Dad said.

"Ernest, shut up," Mom shot back.

He shook his head in annoyance, and I laughed at them bickering. It reminded me of April and me and how neither of us would let the other have the last word.

"What did you cook?" I questioned.

"Mashed potatoes, broccoli, pot roast, yams, and cheesecake."

"It's not Sunday. Why the enormous meal?"

"I figured you could take some home for lunch at work. I talked to Daphne, and she told me about your women fighting in front of the hospital."

"How the hell did she know? She wasn't even there." I sat at the kitchen table as Mom bustled around getting dinner ready.

"Daphne said that Chasity and some woman named April told her about them coming to blows, looking like a hot mess."

"It wasn't that bad."

"Kevin, I raised you better than that, and you're a doctor. Have some decorum with these women. I know you're still dealing with Aaliyah not being here anymore, but that's not an excuse to be out slinging your little thing around to every woman who says hi to you," Mom fussed.

"Eve, leave the boy alone. He takes after his father. I was young once. He needs to explore before settling down again." Ernest kissed her and tapped her thigh.

She smiled, but that only meant she was letting him think she agreed with him. In five minutes, she'd be back to trying to run my life.

"Let's have dinner. Ella, turn the TV off and come help your glam momma," Mom said, calling for Ella to come to the table.

Chapter 10

April

Two weeks later, I had lunch with the girls at the sports bar. I finally wanted some sound advice about what I was doing with Kevin. Chasity, Kyla, and Daphne stared at me, waiting for me to share.

Over the past few weeks, I'd weighed my options and gone on several more dates with Kevin. We'd talked openly about what we expected of each other, and he'd promised that Brianna and Denise would no longer be a problem. I'd worked my regular shifts at the hospital and had no run-ins with Brianna, although I wasn't sure how long that would last.

I drank my second lemon drop martini of the night. We were all dressed in our finest because we planned to go to a lounge afterward and listen to music.

"What's the big news?" Chasity prompted.

"I'm dating Kevin and going to Club Seek as his submissive tomorrow," I blurted.

"I'm happy for you," Kyla said with a smile. "I'm glad you took your time thinking it over and didn't rush anything just to sleep with him."

"I was close to saying no when I witnessed the fight between Brianna and Denise. But Kevin and I talked, and I realized I couldn't hold every petty thing they did against him. But if the shit gets out of hand, I'll be done for sure. The dick may be good, but it's not worth my sanity."

"Have you met Ella?" Daphne asked, dipping a chip into the salsa and taking a bite.

"We've hung out. Ella's a sweet little girl, although I never know what will come out of her mouth, and he spoils her rotten."

Kyla laughed as she sipped on her virgin margarita. "I love Ella. You should see her when she's bossing Warren Jr and Kylan around. They treat her like a little sister."

The server approached with more napkins, and Chasity tapped her margarita glass for another.

"Kevin seems like a jerk sometimes, but he likes you. Don't mind Brianna or Denise. I know they can be difficult, but Kevin had nothing serious with them," Daphne explained.

"Kyla, is there anything I need to know? Were you nervous when you started as a submissive?"

"I wasn't because consent and safety were a priority for both parties, especially the sub. If you decide to turn it into a relationship, be honest about whether you want to continue with the submissive role. Warren takes care of me, and I take care of him," Kyla explained.

"Here's to the submissive lifestyle. May it be everything I hope and include multiple orgasms," I joked, holding my glass up for a toast.

"Did Kevin explain about having a safe word? Some women don't like men with kinks," Kyla said.

"He did, and he told me about punishments by withholding orgasms. A little pain and pleasure combined can elevate your orgasm."

"It's so weird to hear about Kevin being in the lifestyle. Wow! You never really know a person," Daphne stated, sipping her drink.

"You should try it out, Daphne. You might find some enjoyment there." Kyla smirked.

"Benny would never blindfold me or tie me up. I can barely get him to eat my pussy right," Daphne huffed.

Chasity and I laughed, and I waved to the server.

"You ladies need anything else?" our server asked.

"The check would be fine, please," I replied.

Chapter 11

Kevin

few months later.

I told myself this would only be a one-time thing. I'd tried to talk myself out of liking April over the last few months, but I noticed she'd become more open with me lately. After the elevator incident, I couldn't get her off my mind.

When she showed up at Club Seek with Chasity and I removed my mask, our eyes had connected, and fury prevented me from finishing the scene with Roslyn. I told her I'd set up another time for us, but I needed to wrap my mind around the fact that April was stepping into my world after becoming a member.

Like right now. I stood naked in the playroom with April, tied up on the bed. This was our first time playing since she'd visited the club and watched a few more scenes, and she wanted to explore her sexual pleasure. Now she was a member, I'd gathered a few toys—nothing outside the norm that would scare her off.

Seeing her vulnerable state, I wanted to forget about the toys and fuck her until she realized she couldn't control my emotions. I wanted to kick the ass of every guy who'd looked at her the first time she showed up at the club wearing that red dress.

"Do you understand the rules?" I questioned.

I had the room all night. I didn't know her tolerance for pain yet, so I opted out of using cold and hot toys. My last sub loved playing with wax, and she always came undone when I applied ice to her breasts before warming them with my tongue.

"Yes, Sir."

"You understand I'm not a doctor, your boss, or Kevin. I'm your Dom, and you're my Submissive."

"Yes, Sir."

"Good. Have you chosen a safe word?"

Her eyes glowed as she nodded.

I lowered the lighting to enhance the mood. "I need verbal consent, April. You don't usually have a problem letting me know how you feel."

"Thunder," she murmured.

"Does thunder have a significant meaning for you?"

"We've been in a verbal battle from the moment we met. Whenever we clash, it's like driving through a thunderstorm."

I agreed with a nod and moved closer. Leaning into her ear, I whispered, "Let go. Embrace the pleasure, baby." I kissed behind her ear, running a hand along her jaw and down her chest to tweak her nipple.

"Oh!" she gasped.

Her breathing was uneven as I gently squeezed, licking and pinching her nipple. Her eyelashes fluttered.

"Stay with me, baby. We're just getting started."

April was delectable and ready for more intense pleasure.

"Mmm...Yes..." She bit her lip to stifle her cries of delight.

Our eyes locked as I switched to her other breast. She moved against the ropes, and I smiled at the teasing ache of her growing lust.

She stared at me with longing. "I need more, Sir."

"You will in time."

I picked up the mask on the tray and covered her eyes. My heart danced with excitement. "I want you to concentrate and just feel. Don't overthink. Just let go."

Grabbing the feather off the tray, I slowly slid it up and down the soles of her feet.

"Kevin!"

"This will only make it last longer. Remember what to call me?"

"Sorry, Sir."

"Good girl." I maneuvered the feather up her leg and reached for the nipple clamps.

"These are nipple clamps, baby. If you're uncomfortable, let me know, and I'll take them off. Tonight is all about your pleasure, and if something doesn't feel right, use your safe word."

April cried out when I slipped my index finger into her sweet sex as I placed the nipple clamp on one breast and then the other.

"Ah!! God... Sir."

Removing my finger, I licked her essence, moaning at her sweet taste. "Baby, you taste good. I need more."

Lying flat on the bed, I separated her lips with my fingers and probed her sex with my tongue. My aching erection wanted more, but I needed to keep control before we took the next step.

"Fuck!"

"Mmm," I moaned, coating her breast with her wetness, continuing to tweak and squeeze her breast as my lips became familiar with her pussy.

"It's too much... I can't take it, Sir. Ugh! Wait... please." She writhed in place as her orgasm threatened to explode.

"Come for me, baby. Let me hear you," I commanded, French kissing her bottom lips and cupping her breasts until she squirted down my throat.

"Shit! Shit! Shit!" she shouted.

I hovered over her, staring at her flushed cheeks and pouty lips. Her beauty enamored me. Grabbing the condom from my pants pocket, I sheathed my dick. A shudder passed through her as I slid inside. I gripped her hips as she rocked against me, her pussy squeezing my dick. "Baby, you feel so good."

She was close to the brink, and my cock swelled. The hunger inside me could only be sated by her.

"Kevin," she whimpered.

I let out a raw groan as I pulled out of her, removing the condom.

"Open your mouth and your juices off my dick until you get my name right," I told her, guiding my dick into her mouth.

She closed her lips around my dick, and I slid another finger into her pussy. I stood on the side of the bed, pumping slowly into her mouth. She made me ravenous.

"You like that, baby." It was more a statement than a question because her body was reacting beautifully to our play.

She nodded as her pussy wept with need.

"Stop!" I commanded, sliding my dick out and positioning myself at her pussy. "What do you call me?"

"Sir!" she screamed when I pushed through her walls.

"Fuck!" I shouted in a frenzy of need.

The peak of pleasure was on the tip of my dick. Grabbing a handful of sheets, I thrust faster and faster until we came together.

I pulled out of her, removing the ropes on her hands and ankles. Picking her up, I carried her to the bathroom and guided her into the shower. "Relax. Let the hot water ease your muscles."

"Yes, Sir," she whispered.

My feelings for her had nothing to do with her wanting to submit. Our connection went far beyond the pleasure we found at Club Seek.

Chapter 12

April

It was early when Kevin dropped me off at home. He asked to come back once he'd dropped Ella to school. I showered again and pulled on boy shorts, a long shirt, and bunny slippers. Leaving my hair down, I applied lip gloss and went to the kitchen to cook breakfast while waiting for him to arrive. Opening the fridge, I grabbed the orange juice and milk, pouring a glass of both. I didn't know if he liked coffee or tea, so he could choose when he got here.

The doorbell rang as I finished chopping strawberries, grapes, and apples into a bowl. I wiped my hands on the dish towel and headed to the door. Checking the peephole, I bit my bottom lip. Kevin looked sexy in jeans and a T-shirt. I greeted him with a hug, and he held me close, capturing my lips.

"You taste sweet," Kevin moaned through the kiss.

"Thank you, but save that for later," I said, escorting him to the kitchen.

"You prepared all this?" he asked, looking at the pancakes, bacon, toast, and fruit.

I motioned him to sit at my four-seater table. "I did, and I hope you like everything." I sat next to him and offered him coffee or tea.

"Orange juice is fine."

"Sure." I handed it to him.

His hand slid up my thigh and across my back. He leaned over and kissed the top of my shoulder. "Relax. I'm not used to this timid, quiet April."

"It's ironic. I didn't want any of this when I was with my ex."

"Who was your ex?" Kevin questioned, dipping a piece of the bacon in the syrup.

"He's not important," I said, adding strawberries to my pancakes. "Is Ella okay with us dating? I don't want her to think I'm trying to replace her mother."

"She doesn't, and I'd never let that happen. She knows who her mother was. You and I know what this is between us, so don't let anyone get in your head. I know you're hot and cold with me sometimes."

I punched his arm lightly. "Not true!"

He laughed at my outburst. "Girl, you're ready to fight me any minute of the day. I can't tell you how many times Kyla, Daphne, and Chasity wanted to take my head off. Kyla was so pissed that I'd hurt her friend's heart."

I waved him off. "You did not hurt my feelings. Get that out of your head."

"Okay, Rhonda Rousey."

I laughed at his comment. "Are you on call today?"

He shook his head. "I took today off. It's the first Saturday I've had off in a while. You got any plans?"

"I have to go see my parents later today, but I'd like to cook dinner for you and Ella tonight."

"That can be arranged. For now? I want a tour of your place."

"Not much to see. I have an office in the back where I store my drawings for safekeeping."

"What do you draw?"

"You might think it's weird, but I draw my patients."

"I think that's cool."

"We work such long hours and make friendships with our patients. We become like family."

"I know what you mean. Kind of like Mrs. Little. She's all alone. I try to spend time with her, even when I'm not working."

I grabbed our plates and stood, taking them to the sink to wash. Kevin trailed behind me.

"You can relax in the living room. I won't be long."

"I want to help, baby."

"Does it feel weird calling me that? Based on how we got started?"

He shrugged and kissed me.

"No. I figure the best relationships start from chaos. It was my fault, and I own that. I overreacted and dealt with my emotions badly."

"Did you go to Club Seek that night?"

"No."

"Did you see Brianna or Denise that night?"

"April, focus on the now. They're in the past and hold no space in my life. Only you and Ella because that little girl will fight you for her daddy's attention." Kevin laughed.

Laughing, I turned away, getting the water to a pleasant temperature. He grabbed the towel and started drying as I washed. Twenty minutes later, we'd put the food away and watched a movie cuddled up on the couch.

...

Kevin and I fell asleep on the couch. I woke him up four hours later, letting him know I had to leave. We kissed goodbye, and I headed off to my parents' house. They were sitting at the table eating lunch. I stole a fry off my father's plate.

"How is the hospital treating you, baby?"

"It's going okay, Daddy."

"I heard from your fiancé. He wants to try again," my mom informed me.

Hearing his name sparked a headache. We'd ended on bad terms. My mother was supposed to be on my side, so I was pissed that she'd taken his calls. Mom was determined to make me miserable. I didn't know why she wanted me to be with someone who thought so little of me as a person, let alone as a wife. I respected my mother, but liking her was a struggle at times. It was ironic because my father was the complete opposite: cool and laid back. He loved my mom and saw a side of her I didn't.

"Mom, I've moved on. I'm not interested in him."

"Belinda, that boy only wants to knock her up because he needs someone to help him further his career in the church," Dad explained, taking a swig of his lemonade.

"Joe, that is not true," Mom objected. "I talked with his parents, and he misses April. He understands she wants to work, but since his career will keep him busy, it would be good for April to focus on having a family and stop running around with that doctor."

"Kevin's an impressive guy. It took me a little while to

see that side of him, but he doesn't hold me back. In fact, the opposite is true."

"He's a sex fiend!" Mom exclaimed.

"Ma!" I covered my face with my hands, embarrassed. My dad chuckled, and I opened one eye to glare at him.

"That's not funny, Joe. Your child is into deviant things, and that man is the cause of her behaving like a slut."

Dad frowned. "Hold on now, Belinda. That's our daughter you're talking about. Stop throwing stones because you ain't innocent. You wanted to watch some new porn movie the other night, so you can't talk."

I wanted to throw up at my parents discussing sex. I waved my hands frantically for him to shut up. "I'm going to be sick. Please change the subject." I grabbed the glass of water off the table.

"Your father doesn't know what he's talking about. That was a mistake purchased on our cable." Mom lied her way out of him busting her secrets.

"I don't need to hear any more about your and Dad's sex life."

"Anyway, that doctor sounds like he's a righteous guy, and you look happy. Bring him over so we can meet him. How are his parents?" Dad questioned.

"His parents are retired. His daughter, Ella, is adorable and funny. He lost his wife a year ago in a car accident."

"So you're okay with being a stepmom rather than an actual mom," Mom asked, furrowing her brow.

"Why do you make dating someone with a child sound offensive? I'm not her mother and have no plans to become a mother anytime soon. I never said I hated kids or didn't want them. It wasn't in the cards to date someone this early on with a child after getting out of a bad relationship. Kevin understands that Ella and I are friends. That works for us."

"You young girls nowadays have no clue," Mom spat.

"Love the support, Mom. I have to get home to cook dinner. I'll call you guys sometime next week to see if we can all get together," I said, standing to hug and kiss my father. I did the same to my mom before heading off to pick up some groceries. I was cooking dinner for Kevin and Ella. Today was the first time Ella would be in my home, and I wanted her to feel special, so Kevin had told me all the things she liked to eat.

Chapter 13

April

"I thought you had a date tonight," I commented to Chasity as she entered the apartment with takeout.

Chasity placed the Chinese food on the table and pulled out the food trays. "Not tonight. Simon had to work late, and I saw your car in the driveway."

"I went to the grocery store. I still need to cook dinner," I said, curling up on the couch with my wine.

Chasity passed me a plate of rice and vegetables with organ chicken.

"Thanks," I mumbled around a forkful of food.

"You're home early."

"I went to see my parents."

"Everything okay?"

"No. My mom is driving me crazy."

Chasity paused with an egg roll halfway to her mouth. "What happened now?"

I lowered the volume on the TV. "She talked to my ex."

Chasity's eyebrows lifted. "Ex-fiancé?"

"Yeah, and acted like I was crazy for dating Kevin."

"Why?"

"Because she thinks me dating a guy with a kid is stopping me from being a real wife and mom." I emptied my wine glass and poured another.

"Sounds like she crossed some boundaries."

"My mom has no clue what boundaries mean."

"I like Kevin for you."

I smiled, pushing the food around on my plate. "Me too."

"Here's to you and Kevin. You're a grown woman. Everything will be all right." Chasity snickered, popping the eggroll into her mouth.

"Are you staying the night?"

Chasity gathered her trash. "No. I'm going to bed and dreaming of my man."

Chuckling, we continued talking while I cooked dinner and planned a movie. Hearing my phone ping, I picked it up to see a text message.

Kevin: *Miss you. Almost there.*

Me: *I miss you more. Drive safe.*

Kevin: *Once we get Ella to bed, we can have alone time.*

Me: *Chasity is here.*

Kevin: *So it's friends and family night.*

"Tell your boyfriend I said hello," Chasity teased.

I laughed, dropping the spoon on the counter.

Me: *Chasity is pissed that I'm talking to you right now.*

Kevin: *Tell her my bad. We're parking.*

Me: *All right.*

"Sorry. He's about to come up with Ella."

He texted an emoji with its tongue out and a bed, making me blush.

"Look at you blushing," Chasity joked.

I grinned and put the phone aside.

Chapter 14

Kevin

Ella loved hanging out at April's place last night. Chasity hung with us, and Simon was like a big teddy bear with her. I almost couldn't get Ella to bed because my baby had a new favorite person and wanted to hang with Simon all night.

I was with Mrs. Little, checking her temperature. She'd relapsed because someone had fucked up her medication, and now she was on a ventilator. I suspected Brianna but didn't have proof. Daphne told me that Brianna had stayed close to Mrs. Little's room all day and last night. But April's signature was on the medical records, which I knew was a lie because she'd been with me.

If Mrs. Little didn't wake up, I was afraid I'd have to make a decision I didn't want to make. Ella often talked with her on FaceTime, which brought her joy. I knew Daphne was upset that she couldn't be here all the time to watch over everything.

Dropping my pen in my coat pocket, I left her room and went to the nurse's desk.

Brianna smiled at me. "Kevin, do you need me to do anything for you?"

I slapped the charts down on the desk. "You've done enough, Brianna."

"It wasn't me. She was fine when I saw her last time."

"Yeah, okay," Daphne muttered.

"How is everyone doing today?" Denise appeared with a box of donuts.

Her presence shocked me because I'd made it clear I was done with her and Brianna. "What are you doing here?"

"I brought you some snacks. You're a busy man, and as your woman, I need to ensure you're taken care of in every way," Denise announced, running a hand up my chest.

I captured her wrist and pushed her hand away.

"Didn't we make things clear last time? You're not his girlfriend." Brianna jumped up and walked around the nurse's desk to get in Denise's face.

I held my arm out, blocking her. "This is not happening. We're in a hospital, and you two have caused enough problems. Brianna, check on room three twenty. Mr. Sanders should be ready for his medicine."

"Fine. We'll talk when she's gone," Brianna snapped.

"Denise, shouldn't you be at work?"

"I quit. I want to be here for you full-time, baby."

April emerged from the bathroom as Denise hugged my waist.

"Did I miss the party?" she asked through clenched teeth.

"No. Denise was leaving," I muttered.

"No, I wasn't, silly. Daphne, do you want a donut? I

have your favorite, strawberry-filled coconut." Denise ignored all the eyes watching her.

Daphne moved around the nurse's station, glaring at her sister. "Denise, why did you quit working? You love being a realtor."

"I'm not crazy, guys. Kevin, can we go to lunch, please? I have a surprise for you," Denise stated.

Brianna came out of Mr. Sanders' room and headed toward us, bumping April with the medicine cart. "Oops! Sorry, I didn't see you there."

"Brianna, finish your rounds. Daphne, escort Denise from the hospital and let security know she's not allowed back in here unless it's an emergency," I commanded, grabbing April's hand and leading her to my office.

I closed the door behind us and pushed her against it, letting her have all my weight. I yanked her arms above her head and kissed down her neck. "Sorry about them," I apologized with lingering kisses.

"I understand. You're hard to resist," April said breathlessly.

One hand went under her shirt while the other held her wrists. "I only want you, baby. Don't let this change your mind about me. I haven't done anything to provoke this shit show."

April moaned as I squeezed her breast. I wanted to fuck her right here, but I wanted more than thirty minutes.

"Please, Sir," she begged as if reading my thoughts.

I groaned in her ear. "Say it again."

"Sir, please...don't stop."

"Your wish is my command, baby," I told her, sliding my hand into her scrubs and pushing a finger into her tight sex.

"Yes... Oh...Yes."

"I hoped we'd have more time, but we'll have a session at Club Seek tomorrow with no interruptions."

April nodded, and I inserted a second finger. Her release shuddered through her, and I withdrew my fingers, placing them in her mouth so she could taste her essence.

"Go and clean up and be ready for me tomorrow," I told her.

Chapter 15

April

"Stick your tongue out."

I was face down, tied up on a cross, and Kevin was standing naked in front of me. He teased me, easing his dick in and out of my mouth. It was torture, but I knew this was all about the scene. Kevin's head fell back as he massaged my shoulders. Hearing his moans made me wetter by the second. Pleasing him was pleasing me ten times more.

"Just like that, baby."

"Mmm..." I moaned softly. I wanted to touch him and feel his muscular thighs against mine.

"Remember your safe word?"

I nodded.

"Good. That's enough for right now." He caressed my cheek as he slid his dick out of my mouth. He walked over to the tray of toys and picked up the vibrator. "You're familiar with a vibrator, so tonight, we'll have a little fun with it."

He turned it on and placed it against my clit.

"Ah! Sir," I cried out.

"Shush. Just feel it, baby. This is set on low, and now I'm going to add my tongue."

As his tongue eased into my ass, I lost it and tried to break free of the ropes. I was completely naked, legs spread open with him behind me, giving me so much at once that tears filled my eyes. "Please!! Fuck me now."

"You want my tongue or my dick?" He turned the vibrator up, and I almost passed out from the combined sensations.

"Your dick!" I screamed.

"That's good to know." He dropped the vibrator on the floor and slid inside me. His strokes were steady, and our groans filled the room. "Shit, baby. You're so tight," he whispered, his breath hot against my ear. His fingertips traced across my lips.

"Ah! Oh... keep going," I directed.

The slap of our bodies echoing in the room drove me crazy. He hovered over my back, kissing and rubbing my arms and shoulders as he penetrated my walls. Intense pleasure clawed up my spine, and I gasped as my body erupted.

* * *

An hour later, we lay in the bed, cuddling and eating the fruit and chocolate Kevin had sent up.

He ran a hand up my thigh beneath the sheet that covered us, kissing along my neck. "How do you feel?"

"I'm okay. Sore, but good." My happiness woke an answering joy in him.

"I told you to take a shower. It helps with the soreness, baby."

"I know, and I will. I just want to lie with you for a little while."

"We never discussed it, but I want to make this exclusive, you and me."

"Are you asking me to be your girlfriend?" Something foreign melted my heart.

His intense gaze slammed into me. "Girlfriend and Submissive when we're at the club. I don't share, April."

"What about Ella?"

Kevin smiled. "Ella adores you."

"What about your other women?" I chastised, pushing his shoulder gently.

"I haven't been with anyone but you since our first night together. I can't contemplate being with another woman, and I haven't introduced anyone to Ella since Aaliyah died."

"I understand if her death is too painful to talk about."

"It was a freak accident. I blame myself because we argued over the phone, and I never said I love you when we hung up."

"What about Aaliyah's parents?"

"I keep in touch with them, and Ella visits, or they visit us here. I realized I couldn't lock myself away from loving again. Aaliyah wouldn't want me to live my life alone. I'm not cut out for it."

"Do you ever want to get married again?" I questioned.

Kevin shrugged. "I don't know. Honestly, at this moment, I don't, but life can change in a second. What I know is that I want to see where we can go with this." He pointed between us.

"Then we'll take things slow and be exclusive. If one

of us ever feels we need to step back, we'll let the other know, and feelings won't be hurt. Deal?" I held my pinky finger out to seal the deal. It was my go-to thing.

Kevin laughed and entwined his pinky finger with mine, sealing our deal with a kiss.

Chapter 16

Kevin

"Ella, you can't have every shoe in the store, baby."

"Yes, I can, Daddy. April said so," Ella explained.

I had both my girls in the shopping mall with me. April kept looking down at her phone. I didn't know what was going on, but it caused a harsh grimace on her face. Ella was with the sales rep, so I walked over to where April was sitting on the bench.

I clasped a hand on her thigh. "April, what's up?"

"Nothing." She raised her eyes to mine briefly before they dropped to her phone again.

"Has to be something because you're all into your phone and not here with us."

She grunted. "I have a lot on my mind, that's all."

"I need more information than that, love."

April ran a hand through her hair. "It's nothing, Kevin. I'm fine, so drop it. Damn. I'm not one of your other little hoes. I don't need coddling."

"Hold up, where is this coming from?"

"Nothing, I'm sorry. Just having a foul day. Let's grab some lunch and continue shopping."

"Are you sure?"

"Yeah, and I hope you don't mind if I don't come to your place tonight. I feel like being home in my bed."

"We can go to your place instead."

"I appreciate it, but I want to be alone."

"Is this your way of breaking up with me?"

"No. I just need some space."

"You got it." I stood and rejoined Ella. Glancing over my shoulder, I saw that April was absorbed in her phone again.

Ella finally picked out two pairs of shoes she loved. We left the mall and headed for my car. I helped Ella in, but before I could open April's door, she jumped in and locked her door. I had no idea what had caused her change in attitude, but I wasn't about to kiss her ass.

I pulled into traffic and drove to her place. It was probably wise to have some time apart. I turned the music up, and Ella danced in the back. April looked over at me, and I avoided her stare. If she had a problem with me, she needed to speak up. Thirty minutes later, we arrived at her place. I'd barely stopped the car when April reached in the back and rubbed Ella's leg. "Bye, Ella."

"Bye, April." Ella waved.

April was out of the car before I could speak.

"Women," I muttered.

"I'm a woman, Daddy." Ella grinned.

"No, you're my little nugget, and you can never grow up."

She giggled, displaying the dimples in her cheeks.

I started the car back up and drove home. I unlocked the front door, and Ella ran to her room. I placed the bags next to the door, listened to the answerphone messages, and checked the mail. Heading upstairs, I changed into jeans and a T-shirt and started on dinner. Pulling out my phone, I texted April.

Me: *You feeling better?"*

April: *What?"*

Me: *Has your attitude changed, and are you feeling better?*

April: *I don't have an attitude, Kevin.*

Me: *Could have fooled me.*

April: *I'm busy.*

Me: *With whom?*

April sent laughing emojis.

April: *Tell Ella I said goodnight.*

Me: *Is she the only one who gets a good night?*

I placed the pot roast and mashed potatoes on the stove.

April: *Goodnight, Sir.*

Me: *Change that attitude, or I will.*

I closed out the text thread and finished getting dinner.

Chapter 17

April

"That's the problem, Kyla. I think I'm falling in love with him."

"I don't see that as a bad thing." Kyla grabbed an apple from the basket.

We were in the cafeteria, grabbing lunch. Kyla had just finished her checkup with her oncologist, and we'd met for lunch before she had to pick the boys up from school.

"Would that be fair to Ella, though? I don't know if I want to be that full-time motherly presence in her life."

"One thing I've learned is not to push your feelings away. If I'd told Warren how I felt early on, it wouldn't have taken us so long to become a couple," she remarked.

She passed the cashier ten dollars while I pulled out another twenty and paid for my salad and fries. We found a table in the corner and sat down.

"Do you regret becoming a mom?"

"No, never. I always wanted to be a mom. They complete me, and Warren has been so supportive of my career. He wouldn't have cared if I was a stay-at-home mom or working. The only thing he wants is for me to be happy. If Kevin is who you want, don't let him get away."

Someone cleared their throat. I looked up to see Brianna standing beside our table with a harsh glare. "Yes, can I help you?"

Brianna slammed her hand on the table. "Kevin is mine. Find someone else to steal and leave my man alone."

The entire cafeteria went silent, and everyone stared at us. I didn't like confrontation, especially at my place of work. This was one of the reasons I didn't want to commit to Kevin, who'd been involved with Brianna and Denise.

"Brianna, what you and Kevin had was a fling, sweetie."

"That's a lie. We've been dating for six months. I suggest you find someone else to drag into your miserable life."

"And if I don't?"

Then you can find another job," Brianna responded.

"Brianna, enough. Kevin never led you to believe you were in a relationship," Kyla stated.

Brianna folded her arms over her chest. "I know you're her friend, Kyla, but stay out of this."

"Are you threatening me?" I questioned.

"I don't make threats. I make promises."

I chuckled in disbelief and stood. "Listen, girl. You need to focus your energy somewhere else and get you some business. If you ever try to threaten me again, I will kick your ass up and down this cafeteria."

Kyla jumped up, getting in the middle of us. I tried to reach around her, and someone grabbed my wrist.

I looked over my shoulder to see Kevin. "Get off me!"

"What the hell is going on here? I get a page that

you're fighting in the cafeteria?" Kevin demands, grabbing my arms and pulling me behind him.

I pushed him out of the way. "No, your little slut bucket threatened me if I didn't stop seeing you."

"Kevin, I told her the truth. That we were together, and you were at my house the other night," Brianna said.

"I'm not doing this," I hissed. "Kyla, let's go."

"Brianna, stop lying." Kevin reached for me. "April, get back here."

I smacked his hand away. "I have work to do, and wasting my time with you two is not on my agenda."

I turned and walked off with Kyla.

Kyla shook her head. "I don't think she's telling the truth."

"It doesn't matter. I didn't say anything, but I think she's been sending me messages on my phone. The issue with Mrs. Little is under investigation, and the supervisor has been giving me late shifts. When I work those, I'm too exhausted to see Kevin."

"Brianna's uncle is the Executive Director of the hospital, right?" Kyla asked.

"Yeah, so I wouldn't put it past her to try something."

"What did Daphne say?"

"I never told her."

Chapter 18

Kevin

I hadn't seen April in four days. The Executive Director investigated Mrs. Little's medicine mishap and determined that Daphne and I would closely monitor the administering of drugs.

I went to April's place to see what was going on with us since she wasn't returning my calls. I knocked on her door and waited for her to answer. A minute later, the door opened, and she looked like I was the last person she wanted to see.

"Can I come in?"

"No."

"April, you haven't answered my calls. I'm starting to think you don't want to be with me."

"I've avoided you because I'm on suspension until the investigation regarding Mrs. Little is over. Your crazy stalker girlfriends are fucking with my job. So sorry if I'm not in the best mood and don't want to see your face right now," April snapped.

I blocked her attempt to slam the door in my face.

"I'm working with Daphne to get things cleared up faster."

"Don't do me any favors. This wouldn't have happened if you hadn't slept around with so many bitches."

"The only person I've slept with is you! Stop acting crazy and listen to me, goddamn it!" I shouted, pushing my way inside.

"Go away!"

"No!"

"I don't care what you do with them anymore. I'm over this soap opera of fighting for your heart. They can have you."

"You don't mean that, baby. I'm sorry. I promise you won't lose your job."

"You can't promise that. I'm already on suspension until further notice because of the cafeteria incident."

"Do you want to talk about what happened?"

"No. Please go."

"Can I have a kiss?"

"No. Leave, and don't come back."

I gripped her arm and pulled her against me, capturing her lips. I squeezed her ass, and she lifted her arms around my neck. I walked her backward as she unbuckled my pants. Pulling her shorts down, I spun her around, bent her over the couch, and slid inside her wet pussy.

"Ah!" April panted as I eased out and thrust inside.

I picked up my pace and gripped the back of her neck. "Fuck!"

"Ugh... Sir... Yes."

I continued hitting her deep until we both orgasmed, and I emptied my seed inside her. I'd forgotten all about wearing a condom. I slid out of her, pulling my pants up while she tugged her shorts back up.

"I can't do this anymore, Kevin."

"What?"

"All the drama. I left all that behind in my past, and I can't do it in a new relationship. They can have you." April wiped her tears and walked away, leaving me stunned.

Chapter 19

April

I was reinstated at the hospital after a two-week suspension. I heard they'd also suspended Brianna, but she was back, working on a different floor. Daphne said that Denise hadn't been back, and I was happy not to see either woman.

Things weren't great with my mom. Brianna's aunt went to the same church as my parents, so it wasn't long before my breakup with Kevin was the talk of the neighborhood. Mom called, accusing me of embarrassing the family because of a man. My dad tried to calm her down, to no avail.

Kyla and Warren were throwing a party today and invited me over. Kyla hadn't told me if Kevin would be there, but I hoped he stayed away. It was bad enough that we worked in the same hospital. The only silver lining was that Chasity and I were now working together on the kid's wing.

I finished my rounds and headed to the staff room.

"Hey, girl, are you ready?" Chasity asked.

"Yeah, let me grab my bag."

I closed my locker and followed Chasity out of the staff room.

"Did you cook anything for today?" Chasity asked.

"No. I was going to pick up something. I know Warren and the kids loved the chocolate cake last time we all had dinner." I reached my car in the parking lot and slid inside, spotting a note on the windshield. I pulled it off and read it, my brows furrowing at the words.

You've got him for now, but don't get too comfortable, bitch!

I balled the paper up and threw it away. As usual, Brianna was deluded. I wasn't even with Kevin anymore.

"You ready?" Chasity questioned, throwing her purse in the back seat.

"Yep."

I started the car and reversed out of the parking space, holding my badge up at the security gate. It opened, and I drove toward home. I put on some Megan Thee Stallion. I needed to get back to my old self.

"Ooh, that's my song. Turn that up. *Hot Girl Summer!*" Chasity tried to twerk in her seat.

I laughed at her and hyped her up by pretending to pass her a microphone. We chuckled all the way home.

An hour later, we arrived at Kyla and Warren's place. Cars were lined up, so we parked in front of the neighbor's house. I carried a cake I bought from the store while Chasity held two pies. I wore a jumpsuit short set, and she wore wide pants with sandals and a top with a cutout back out, showing off her curves.

"I'm surprised Simon let you out of the house looking so cute."

"Simon's my boyfriend, not my daddy," Chasity teased.

"That's what I like to hear. Men think they can run us, and we have to agree with anything they say. No, ma'am. Not today, buddy boy."

The door flew open, and Warren Jr. ran toward us. "Auntie April! What did you bring us?"

"Hey, Warren Jr. Give me a kiss." I tried to kiss his cheek, and he wiped it off.

"Warren Jr., that's rude," Kyla said, standing at the door with Ella next to her.

"Sorry, Mom," Warren Jr. muttered, walking into the house.

"That's okay, Kyla. He's a growing boy, and it's not cool to get kisses anymore," I said, bending down to hug Ella.

"Ella, your April is here." Kyla pointed at me.

"Hi, April," Ella greeted before running off with Warren Jr.

"These kids don't care unless you're candy or video games. Otherwise, they have no use for you." I laughed, stepping inside.

Kyla grabbed the cake, and I followed her into the kitchen.

Chapter 20

April

"Everybody's in the backyard. The food is on the grill, so don't hesitate to make a plate and meet some new friends," Kyla said.

"Thanks, Kyla. Your home is beautiful," Chasity replied, placing her pies next to the cake.

"I got a clean bill of health again, so we're celebrating with a barbeque."

"Yes, congrats. April told me earlier today at work," Chasity announced.

"How is work?" Kyla asked. "I know you told me the investigation was over, and you're on a new shift schedule and floor."

Kyla passed us a Coke, and I opened mine, almost finishing the entire thing. I was nervous about running into Kevin.

"He's not here, so you can relax," Kyla said.

"Is it that obvious?" I joked.

"Yep. So, how are things between you two? Last time we talked, you'd broken up."

I sighed, sitting next to Chasity at the kitchen island.

"We did. I was constantly dealing with women who didn't care what they did to get his attention. One was texting me and blocking her name, but I knew who it was. There's also a good chance she tried to sabotage me at work. I can't prove it, but I think she gave a patient too much medication and forged my name."

The door opened, and Warren walked in wearing shorts and a matching shirt with Warren Jr. and Kylan's names across the chest. I noticed Kyla was wearing the same and had a new short blonde pixie cut.

"When did you change your hair?" I questioned.

"After I got the news from my oncologist. I needed a change. Warren loves me with any style, so I didn't have to worry about my man being turned off by the new setup. Probably helps us role-play more than anything," Kyla joked, and Warren smacked her on the ass.

"Okay, you two. We don't need a scene right here," I said, waving Warren off as he stared lustfully at his wife.

"Warren, what did you cook?" Chasity asked, changing the subject.

"I put burgers, hot dogs, and steaks on the grill. Plus, chips, coleslaw, potato salad, and pizza were delivered a few minutes ago," Warren replied.

Chasity and I stood, heading outside with them. They had a huge backyard that Warren redesigned with a garden for Kyla, a pool, and a guesthouse.

"You guys, this is gorgeous. I love the garden area." I pointed to the blooming flowers.

"I started a few weeks ago, and I'm getting the boys involved," Kyla stated.

"Don't be shy. Grab anything you want. We have plenty for everybody," Warren invited.

"Is that Ian and Devon over there?" I questioned.

Kyla nodded.

"Wow!" Chasity said.

"Is that Simon over there, Chasity?" I asked.

"Yeah, and look at that bimbo in his face!" Chasity hissed, walking off to confront him.

Kyla and I chuckled. Chasity was quick to get angry with Simon when he was jealous, but she did the same thing the second he was seen talking to another woman.

"Those two deserve each other," Kyla said.

"I agree," I replied.

I picked up a plate and scooped some potato salad, coleslaw, and a hotdog onto my plate.

"Let's go and watch the kids in the pool," Kyla suggested.

Chapter 21

Kevin

April was shocked to see me, but I didn't care. Warren called me and asked if I wanted to come and chill at the party. Ella was having fun, and he knew I hadn't been around anyone since April ended things.

I'd replayed my steps throughout our relationship over the past months. It was my fault. I hadn't done enough to remove Denise and Brianna from the picture. It almost cost April her job, and Ella was mad at me because she couldn't see April as much as she wanted.

I headed into the house and noticed a few teenagers playing video games in the front living room. They waved at me, and I nodded, going toward the kitchen. Hearing laughter and kids playing, I stood at the door, watching my friends have a good time. I'd wanted to invite my parents, but they were hanging with friends who'd come to town.

Pushing the door open, I strode to Warren and the guys standing by the grill.

"Hey, man. Glad you could make it," Warren greeted.

"I wouldn't miss this for anything. How was my little nugget?" I asked.

"You know Ella. She ran everything. It had to be specifically how she wanted with the bright pink balloons, and the tablecloths had to coordinate with her outfit. I said, 'Ella, the party is for Auntie Kyla.'"

"And what did my baby say?"

"She said, 'Uncle Warren, if I'm happy, Auntie Kyla is happy. It's a woman thing.'" Warren mimicked Ella's voice and stance with his hands on his hips.

All the guys burst out laughing. I knew Ella would say something like that.

"She's something else," I said affectionately.

"She really is, and it makes me want to have another one day," Warren stated.

"How is she doing?"

"Who? Kyla or April?" Warren questioned, turning the meat over on the grill.

"I know Kyla is good. I see April has a smile on her face."

"Partially because of the kids, and partially because she stays busy with work and not thinking about anything else. I have reliable sources who say she misses you."

"I miss her too," I groaned, running a hand down my face.

"Go talk to her. Maybe the kids have softened her up."

"What did you do with Kyla?"

"I forced her to sign a contract to move in with me when I found out about her cancer. We got to know each other, and we grew into something more," Warren explained.

"Send me one of those contracts because I refuse to go another night without April beside me."

"Go get your woman," Warren said, clapping me on the back.

I made my way over to the women and kids playing.

"Daddy!" Ella screamed and ran into my arms.

I scooped her up and kissed her cheek before placing her back on the ground. "Hey, nugget. Can you give April and me a second to talk?"

"Are you going to apologize?" Ella questioned.

I heard a loud gasp and looked up to see April standing from her seat. She was wearing a jumpsuit that clung to her shapely thighs. I licked my lips, remembering the last time we were intimate and how those thighs felt wrapped around my waist as I plunged into her wet sheath.

"Ella, you don't have to worry about your daddy and me. We're fine, nugget," April explained, bending to her level.

"Will you come home with me? I miss you," Ella said, wrapping her arms around April's neck.

April picked her up and rubbed her back.

"Can we talk in the house? Please?" I asked.

April nodded, following behind me. She held Ella on her hip as we walked into the second bedroom.

"You tired, little nugget?" I questioned.

Ella nodded as she yawned and rubbed her eyes. I took her from April and put her on the bed, slipping her shoes off and covering her up to take a nap until I was ready to leave.

Chapter 22

April

I wanted to be mad at this man, but I also wanted to run into his arms and forget everything that had happened.

"I need you to understand. What happened was my fault. I didn't see how my choices affected you. I guess I was expecting things to magically be good because I was never that deep with those women. I love you, April, and I want this, however you'll have me. Let me make it up to you. Move in with me and Ella."

"Kevin... I don't know if that's a good idea.

"A bad idea is letting this go and not exploring how our lives can be better together."

"Are you talking out of desperation or because you truly want this? Because the thought of moving in with a guy after he fucked me over doesn't appeal to me."

"I'll have a lifetime to make up for that. Ella loves you, and I haven't been able to eat, think, or sleep without you next to me."

"Brianna was texting me and sending pictures of you together."

"Why didn't you tell me sooner?"

"I thought I could handle it myself and block her because I trusted you. But then she started messing with my job and trying to get me fired, and I'd had enough of Kevin Haven's wicked harem," I joked.

"The only woman I want is you, baby. Come home," Kevin begged, caressing my cheek.

"Have you gone to Club Seek since we broke up?"

"No. Sex was the last thing on my mind if it wasn't with you," Kevin confessed.

I knew he was telling the truth because he never took his eyes off me.

"Ella okay with me moving in? She's the woman of the house."

"It was her idea."

"Stop lying." I chuckled.

"I explained everything to the Hospital Administrator. Brianna was fired. She fucked up too many times, and her uncle kept covering it up, so he was also fired."

"Damn. I wonder who they'll get to take on his position."

"They're looking at replacements, but that's not our problem. I want you with me at home, in my bed every night. Driving to work together and all the mushy things that couples do."

I scanned his eyes. "Even at Club Seek?"

He sank to his knees, and I covered my mouth in shock. *Is he proposing?*

"Calm down, I'm not proposing yet," he joked.

I slapped his arm. "Whatever."

"April Benson, will you please resume your role as my sub at Club Seek and my girlfriend at home?"

These past months had changed me for the better,

and I knew I couldn't let Kevin and Ella go, even when his little tribe of women wanted to break us up. I should've known better because I'd dealt with that type with my ex. Being strong was my best trait, but I'd let Kevin down and thought the worst of him. I'd spend the rest of my life showing him the love he'd shown me.

I grinned, wanting to fuck him right here, ring or not.

Chapter 23

Kevin

April grinned. "I'd love to be your submissive. Let's go home and celebrate."

I pushed her back on the bed and kissed her. "You just made me a happy man. Thank you, baby."

We heard a loud crash, and I jumped out of her hold. I ran to the living room to see the front window busted.

"Who the hell would throw a damn brick through a window?" Warren demanded.

Mrs. Cooperson, his elderly neighbor, walked over in a rush. "Warren, I saw the whole thing. I was out walking with Piper, and a crazy woman stepped out of her car. I wasn't too far from your house."

"Is there a note?" I asked.

"Someone wrote 'Fuck you, Kevin' with a black sharpie across the brick."

"Thanks, Mrs. Cooperson. You need me to walk you and Piper home?" Warren asked.

"No. I have my pepper spray. I'm fine, Warren. Have a good night," Mrs. Cooperson said.

"I'll file a police report. She's never been to my house

before and couldn't have known where you live unless..." I stopped as another thought crossed my mind. With the shit Brianna had already pulled, I wouldn't put it past her at this point, but she had crossed a huge line if what I was thinking was true.

"Unless what?" Kyla asked.

"Your medical records," April said.

"Had to be the only way. I worked today, and she was packing up her things. April, we need to get some of your things before we head home." I made a note to mention it to Daphne. She could have the IT department look into whether someone had logged into a patient's medical records. If Brianna had done that, she would be in a world of legal trouble. I'd press Warren and Kyla to do whatever they had to in order to make her pay.

"Do you want to take my car?" Warren questioned.

"We can take you guys, Simon said, wrapping his arm around Chasity and kissing her forehead. "Chasity is my priority, and I'll be damned if someone causes her harm. I'm following behind you."

"Let me get Ella, and we'll head to my place so I can get a few things," April said.

"Well, at least she's out of your lives for good now that the hospital fired her," Kyla commented.

"That girl needs help," I said, taking Ella out of April's arms.

"Thanks for having me, Kyla and Warren. I'm sorry about all this craziness. I never wanted all this on your doorstep," April said.

"No worries. We've been through our share of drama. Take care of yourself, and call me if you need anything," Kyla said, hugging April and then me.

I shook hands with Warren, and we headed to my car,

where I buckled a sleeping Ella into her car seat. April waited for me, and I opened the passenger door and helped her inside. I drove toward April's place to gather her things. Noticing Simon up ahead with Chasity in the car, I honked my horn to let them know we were ready.

I was ready to start a fresh life with the woman I loved. Aaliyah placed an angel in my life, and while I would never forget her or the love we shared, it was time for me to move on.

After we finished putting some of April's things away, we gave Ella a bath. She ended up passing out without me kissing her goodnight. April and I showered, and I drifted off to sleep with her in my arms, dreaming about our family's future.

Chapter 24

April

Three months later.

I didn't know how Kevin would take me being pregnant. With my blossoming relationship with Ella, I didn't want to be out of her life if we didn't make it as a couple. Maybe co-parenting would be something he'd be okay with.

We finally started working through our issues with his frequent women constantly fighting for his attention and me learning more about his world in the BDSM lifestyle. I wasn't sure if he'd want to continue taking me there. I wiped a tear away and slid out of the bathroom after dropping the pregnancy test in the trash.

"What did it say?" Kyla questioned, looking gleeful that I could be with child.

"You have room for another godchild?" I asked, biting down on my bottom lip. I never expected to get pregnant, let alone be a stepmom. My life had completely changed in the last few months, and I had no one to blame but myself.

"OMG! April, I'm so happy for you. We're happy, right?"

I sat on the edge of my bed in my apartment. I still hadn't moved all of my things into Kevin's place. A small part of me was reluctant to give up everything to move in with a ready-made family. "Honestly, I don't know. I never saw myself as a mother."

"How do you feel about Ella?"

"I love Ella. She makes loving her easy," I answered, falling back on the bed and sighing in exhaustion. I just finished working another twelve-hour shift.

"Then this new baby will do the same because you both created it out of love. I remember fighting my feelings for Warren. I didn't believe I could make him happy after battling cancer. I didn't think I could feel like a woman again, let alone be a wife and a mother to his children," Kyla reminded me as she picked up the remote and turned on the television in my room.

"I'm not sure if we conceived this baby through love. I think it was anger that turned into lust," I protested, looking around and remembering our first night together in my bedroom.

The things Kevin did to my body had me craving his touch. Discovering an alternative lifestyle at Club Seek was a challenge I wasn't completely comfortable with. As time went on, I learned to trust Kevin, let go of my control, and own my pleasure. Relinquishing that power gave me control beyond my expectations.

"You need to tell him about the baby and talk honestly about what you both want. I'm ready to start planning a baby shower."

"Oh, my God, Kyla. I literally just found out. Please don't turn into one of those friends who plans out every milestone of having a baby. Give me a few days to come to terms with being pregnant."

Kyla stood and pulled her purse over her shoulder before turning off the TV. "Let's go out to eat and shop. It'll help clear your mind. Maybe we should stop by your parent's place?"

"I can go shopping and get some things for dinner. I need to pick up Ella from Kevin's parents' house. Do you want to tag along or meet me at the mall?"

"We can pick up my kids first and swing by to get Ella. The kids would love to hang out since it's the week-end," Kyla suggested.

"Okay. Let me use the bathroom and throw some water on my face. I probably look crazy, and I'd rather not have Kevin's mom suspect something anything."

Heading to the bathroom, I grabbed a face towel off the rack stand. I washed my face, brushed my teeth, and pulled my hair into a ponytail before adding a little mascara and clear lip gloss. I left the bathroom, grabbed my sandals from my closet, and picked up my purse and jacket. As I followed Kyla out the front door, Chasity came in with a bag of groceries, talking on her cell phone.

"Hold on, Denise. He made it clear you two were not serious. I'll call you back."

"You can't choose your family, honey." I chuckled.

Chasity tossed her phone in her pocket. "I think she's lost her mind over some dick."

"Dick that she'll never see again. What are you doing today? We're about to pick the kids up and head to the mall," I explained, walking to the passenger side of Kyla's car and opening the door.

"I have a date with Simon. Supposed to be movie

night and cuddling. You look weird. Are you all right?" she questioned, waving her hand in front of my face.

"I'm fine. I'll call you tomorrow and we can talk and catch up. Maybe have a girl's day after you spend time with your man."

"Okay. Have fun and tell the kids that Auntie Chasity says hello."

We said goodbye, and I climbed in the car with Kyla.

Thirty minutes later, the kids were in the car.

"Mommy, Bucky ate my new shoes," Warren Jr. said, looking somber.

"Did you leave your shoes out, Warren Jr.? You know Bucky loves new toys, and he probably thought it was a toy," Kyla explained, turning into Kevin's parents' street.

"He ate my shoes, too, Mommy," Kylan stated.

Both boys were adorable, and they'd grown so much from the pictures Kyla showed me when they were first adopted. They kept in touch with Sister Patrice, and the Baptist Memorial Hospital had started doing volunteer work, flying doctors and nurses over to give the kids routine checkups. I told them the next time they decided to do the trip, I would love to go for a few weeks and help contribute. Kyla sent donations they'd accumulated from events organized by TN Seal Security.

Kyla parked in front of the Havens' home, and I got out and opened Warren Jr.'s door while Kyla helped Kylan. I knocked on the front door, and a few seconds later, I heard someone yell that it was open.

Ernest was sitting with Ella in the living watching *Frozen*, and Warren Jr. and Kylan ran over to sit next to her. Ernest started to rise from his recliner, but I waved at him to stay seated and bent to hug him.

"Hi, Ernest. How are you doing?"

"I'm good, April. Is my son treating you right?" he asked, winking at me.

I giggled because the old man was a big flirt like his son. "Yes. Kevin is fine besides the usual craziness I have to deal with at work."

"Ernest, who are you talking to out here?" Eve questioned, entering the living. She was wearing her glasses and gardening gear.

"Hi, Eve. We decided to scoop up Ella and head to the mall," I told her.

"Yeah, the mall! Can I get the new Barbie doll?" Ella ran to me and wrapped her arms around my legs.

I rubbed her back and tapped the end of her nose. "Can you say hi to Mrs. Kyla and the boys, little nugget?"

"Hi, Mrs. Kyla. Hi, Warren Jr. and Kylan. You want to see my treehouse in the backyard?" Ella asked, tugging them outside.

The four adults laughed at her bossy nature.

"She'll be a handful when she gets a boyfriend," I announced.

"That's because her father and grandfather spoil her rotten," Eve explained, sitting on the edge of the recliner.

Ernest rubbed her thigh. "The Haven charm works for everybody, baby."

"That's so true." Eve giggled. "How are you doing, Kyla? I spoke with Warren about some renovations on our home. He's coming to do a walk-through of our place some time next month."

"He's doing good, Eve. I know he wants some of your famous sweet potato pie, so we may have to come here for Sunday dinner one day. I hear it's all the rage. My boys love spending time here." Kyla chuckled, sitting on the couch.

"One day, I'll teach you my tips. Tell my son to call me when he gets home. April, can I talk to you in the kitchen?" Eve asked, standing and walking off.

I hesitated, and Kyla nodded for me to follow behind her. Entering the kitchen, I went to the fridge, grabbed a bottle of water, and sat at the island.

"You look a little off today. Tell Momma Eve what's going on, and don't lie because I can tell something is running around in your head."

I chugged down half the bottle of water. "I'm pregnant," I whispered, scratching the back of my neck.

"I knew it!" She jumped up excitedly, clapped her hands, and reached over to hug me.

"How did you know?"

"The last time I saw you, you looked a little fuller in the hips, but I didn't want to say anything. I'm happy to have another grandbaby. Hopefully, this will lead you two down the aisle after the fiasco with those other women," Eve said dramatically, alluding to Denise and Brianna's attempts to break us up. Technically, they did until I got my shit together.

"Kevin doesn't know yet," I informed her.

"You're planning on keeping it, right?" she probed, narrowing her eyes at me.

"I am, even if Kevin isn't happy about another baby."

"Why would Kevin not be happy? You two made up, and you started moving your things into his house, right?"

"I did, and we're making a commitment to each other. I don't want him to feel we're moving too fast now we've decided to move in together. Our careers are so busy, and he has Ella. I don't want her to feel like she's being pushed aside."

"Ella will be fine. Have you not noticed she follows

your every move? Aaliyah would be proud of how Ella is growing up and the people surrounding her. You've known me long enough to know that I wouldn't approve of just anyone around my grandbaby. So, you've won me over, and Ella will be excited about becoming a big sister."

"Thanks, Eve. I'll have Kevin call you when we get back home."

"No worries. My lips are sealed until then." She kissed my cheek and rubbed my stomach.

Chapter 25

April

I went to the backyard and called for Ella and the boys. They ran toward me, and we left the house for the mall. Soon after, Ella was trying on shoes in the Nike store next to Warren Jr and Kylan. I stood next to Kyla as she talked to the store clerk.

"Can I get two pairs of Jordans in a size eight and ten, please?" Kyla asked.

"Thought that was you," I heard someone say behind me.

I looked over my shoulder to see Brianna with two other women holding shopping bags.

She smacked her lips and placed her hands on her hips. "Kevin left me for you. I don't see it."

Her friends nodded and laughed.

"That's good because it's not about what *you* see, it's what *he* sees and comes home to every night. He loves it, or I wouldn't be living with him," I said calmly, closing the distance between us.

Kyla reached out and pulled me back. "April, ignore her."

"Yeah, do what your friend says. I'd hate to call the police on you for assaulting me," Brianna sneered as she tried to instigate something more than verbal sparring.

"You're not worth my oxygen. Don't forget the restraining order says to stay a hundred feet away. Have a marvelous day, Brianna." I waved her off and went back to Ella.

"Bitch," Brianna muttered over her shoulder.

I shook my head in frustration. If I weren't pregnant, I'd kick her ass, but I knew it would piss Kevin off if I fought in front of Ella and set a bad example.

"Remember, you have the house, the man, and the baby," Kyla reminded me softly. "He never gave her an ounce of what he's given you."

I thanked her with a hug.

"I like these, April." Ella jumped up and danced, swaying her hips from side to side. We all laughed, and I nodded.

"All right. We have a few more stores to check out," I called out, taking the shoes to the counter to purchase.

Taking my wallet out of my purse, I heard my phone vibrate and picked it up.

Kevin: *When are my girls coming home?*

Me: *Aww, you miss us?*

Kevin: *Of course I do, and my baby too.*

Me: *I'm at the mall. We'll be done soon.*

Kevin: *Purchase something sexy for me, baby.*

Me: *Lol! I need to after you ripped everything.*

Kevin: *You know it never stays on long. Get the edible panties I like.*

"Thank you," I told the sales clerk, grabbing the

receipt. Looking back down at my phone, I continued to reply to his messages.

Me: *I'll be home soon, Sir.*

Kevin: *Now I'm hard.*

Me: *I can already taste you.*

Kevin: *Don't play with me.*

Me: *I like to play with you.*

Ella captured my hand to walk beside me. She danced, and I laughed at her joy. Warren Jr. ran in front of us, and Ella played with him behind the poster wall. Closing out of my messages, I saw Kyla motioning toward the food court.

"Pizza!" the kids screamed, running to the pizza pan restaurant.

"Ella, I'm cooking dinner tonight. You can get one or two slices, little nugget." I smooth a hand over her curly hair, surprisingly still in the ponytail I put it in this morning.

"Okay," Ella replied.

"Warren Jr. and Kylan, you can split a medium pizza, and we'll take a second one for Daddy," Kyla said, ordering three pizzas.

I reached into my purse and gave her a twenty-dollar bill for Ella's half. Kyla waved me off, but I stuck out my tongue and tucked it in her purse.

"Three pizzas to go?" the pizza server confirmed.

"Yes," Kyla and I answered at the same time.

Standing off to the side, we waited for the pizzas, and I spotted Denise laughing with an unknown guy on her arm.

"I guess she wasn't so in love with Kevin after all," I muttered.

"Isn't that Denise?" Kyla questioned. "What did Kevin ever see in her?"

"I ask him that all the time. The number of women he went through after Aaliyah passed away was ridiculous. I think he was trying not to deal with the pain or admit he needed to talk with a therapist," I said, thanking the cashier and grabbing the pizza for Ella.

We went to the car, loaded the kids inside with the pizzas, and headed home.

Thirty minutes later, Kyla parked in front of Kevin's house. I helped Ella out of the back and grabbed her shopping bags.

"Daddy! I'm home," Ella shouted, running into Kevin's arms where he sat on the couch.

I followed behind her and kissed him on the lips. He grasped my chin, holding me for a longer kiss.

I almost tripped with the pizza in my hand. "Babe, let me put the pizza away."

"Hurry up and go change. I got us a movie to watch," Kevin explained.

"Ella, go wash your hands, please. I was supposed to make dinner, but Kyla gave us a whole pizza."

"That's fine. You've worked nonstop and need to relax. Pizza is fine," Kevin insisted, pulling my feet onto his lap as I sat beside him.

I sighed as he massaged my feet. "How was work for you today? I didn't get to see you much."

"Mrs. Little didn't make it. I need to figure out how to get in touch with her family. I'm planning on paying for the funeral."

I leaned up and pulled him into a hug. "I'm sorry. What do you need me to do?"

"Honestly, you moving in here and giving me a second chance is all I need," Kevin answered.

"That will be done ASAP. I spend more time here than at my place, so it makes sense for me to move in with you."

"That's what I like to hear. Give me a kiss."

"Mmm..." I cupped his chin, placing a single kiss on his lips.

He gripped my butt. "Keep making noises like that, and Ella's going to hear us," he said, kissing my neck.

He slid his hand under my shirt, and I gasped as he tweaked my nipple. Our breath became labored as he pressed me back on the couch.

"Ew... Daddy, get a room," Ella joked, running back inside.

"Little nugget, you have a TV in your room. How about you eat your pizza there?" Kevin pleaded.

Ella shook her head. "I want to watch a movie here."

I laughed at his grumpy expression and murmured, "We have the rest of the night to talk. Let her watch the movie." I turned to Elle. "What movie did you get?"

"I see what this is. You girls are ganging up on me. Ella, remember you're going to want to go shopping soon," Kevin stated, folding his arm over his chest with a playful pout.

"That's okay, Daddy. April's a better shopper, anyway," Ella told him.

I laughed as I pushed off the couch to change into something more comfortable.

"What did you do to my daughter?" Kevin demanded, pointing over his shoulder as he followed me to the bedroom.

"Sir, I didn't do anything to her besides become her

friend," I said softly, grabbing a t-shirt and leggings to shower. I headed to the bathroom and turned on the shower. Kevin narrowed his eyes on me. "What are you staring at?" I questioned.

"Something's different about you. You seem more relaxed than usual and not as guarded," he observed, pulling me close.

Chapter 26

Kevin

April always challenged me, whether it was at work or at home. This new laid-back attitude raised a red flag.

I ran a hand down her back and cupped her ass cheek. "What's going on?"

"I'm fine." She tried to move out of my arms.

"You can lie to everyone else, but not to me. We made a pact when we got back together to be honest and communicate. I'm not messing with other women. I love you and only you, April."

"I'm pregnant," she blurted.

I froze. "You're pregnant? With my baby?"

"Of course, it's yours, Kevin." She tried to jerk out of my hold.

I tightened my grip. "Calm down. I didn't mean it like that. I'm just...Wow! Are you sure you're pregnant? How far along?"

"I took the test at home earlier with Kyla and haven't gone to the doctor yet. I felt weird the other day and couldn't keep any food down, so Kyla came over with two tests."

"Damn."

"I'm not expecting you to be there for my baby. We can co-parent. I know you weren't looking to knock me up."

"April, quit putting words in my mouth. Your ass is moving in with me, which means everything that comes with you. If I'm going to be a father again, you have no choice but to deal with me, and I'm not letting you go."

"What about Ella? You know she enjoys being the only kid, and you've spoiled her." April chuckled at her comment.

I closed my eyes. I'd come to terms with moving on with my life with April. Part of me would always love Aaliyah, but I was holding a new start in my arms. I'd been reckless with women after losing Aaliyah and made poor choices regarding Brianna and Denise.

"You and Ella are the only things I care about. Nothing and no one will change that."

"I told your mom. Well, she pried it out of me when I picked up Ella today."

"Eve could get an innocent man to plead guilty with just a look. Take a shower. I'll be waiting in the bedroom."

"What about the movie?"

"Ella will be fine. I want to spend some time with you." I left her in the bathroom to get cleaned up.

Stepping into the living room, I set the movie up for Ella and kissed her forehead. She giggled and took a bite of her pizza. I headed to the kitchen and opened the fridge, pulling out a bowl of vegetable soup. I reheated a small portion and grabbed two bottles of water. Setting everything on the tray, I added crackers and fruit, put my phone on silent, and carried it into the bedroom.

April was lounging on the bed with a towel around her waist.

"I thought you were going to get dressed in the T-shirt and leggings?"

"I am, but I forgot my lotion."

"Let me take care of you, baby." I placed the tray down and took the bottle of lotion out of her hands, motioning for her to turn on her stomach.

I squeezed a small amount in my hand, and April tossed the towel on the floor. I had to grit my teeth and think of something else as my dick sprang to life. Her plump ass was calling my name, begging for my handprint.

April moaned as I rubbed the lotion into her shoulders and back. "Sir, you have magical hands."

I kissed the back of her neck. "I have a lot of magical things."

"I know. I can feel one of them poking me in the butt."

"You shouldn't be so damn sexy."

"Thank you, baby."

"Put some clothes on and eat this soup. I'll check on Ella again, and then we're in for the rest of the night."

April nodded and picked up her shirt off the chair. We stayed in the bedroom and watched movies for the rest of the night until Ella fell asleep in the living room.

...

April and I went to her doctor's office for an ultrasound the next day. The doctor stepped out of the room to let her get dressed and check over her blood work. Doctor Latrice and I worked through residency together, and I knew she'd be the perfect person for us to see. Didn't hurt that she was a floor above the ER for easy access to the maternity ward.

April sat on my lap, her fingers tangling in my hair, reminding me I needed a haircut.

"So, April, it looks like you're three months along," Doctor Latrice said when she returned to the room.

"Three months! I'm not even showing," April remarked, rubbing her stomach.

"Don't stress yourself out. It can happen sometimes. Here's a prescription for prenatal vitamins. I want you to get more rest and eat healthy," Doctor Latrice instructed.

"Will I be fine to work?" April asked, standing to grab the paperwork.

"No more twelve-hour shifts, but you can still work," Doctor Latrice advised, printing out the sonogram photo.

"She won't be, Doc. I'll ensure she cuts down at work," I stated, reaching for her hand.

"Congratulations. I'm so happy for you both, and please don't drive her crazy," Doctor Latrice joked.

"Too late for that. He made me oatmeal and tea this morning," April fussed and rolled her eyes at me.

I kissed her forehead, and we left the doctor's office. We stopped at the front desk to make another appointment before heading out for lunch. I held the door open, letting April walk ahead of me to the car, and opened her passenger door. She slid inside, and I jogged over to the driver's side, backing out of the parking space and pulling into traffic.

"Where do you want to eat?" April asked.

"How about we go check in with your parents?"

"Lord, I already know my mother is going to piss me off," April mumbled.

"Why do you say that?"

"She's old-fashioned, and I haven't told her we've moved in together."

"April, you're a grown woman."

"I know, but Belinda Benson is the type to hound you until you agree to do whatever she says."

"I'm not scared of your mother. She can get on board or not." I shrugged, not caring either way.

Turning off the freeway, I parked in front of her parents' house ten minutes later. I got out and helped April out of the car, and we held hands as we went to the door and knocked.

Her mother answered, wearing an apron. "What are you two doing here?"

"Hi, Mom. We were hungry and wanted to see what you cooked." April released my hand to hug her mother.

"I see," Belinda said, stepping to the side to let us inside.

"How are you, Belinda?" I asked politely.

"I'm good, Kevin. How are you doing?"

"Doing okay."

April removed her jacket, following behind her to the couch. "Where's Dad?"

"He's still asleep. I had him cleaning out the garage earlier today. Are you staying for lunch?"

"Yeah. What did you cook?"

"Fish, coleslaw, cornbread, green beans, and salad."

"Oh, I want some fish." April clapped her hands.

"Remember your diet, April," I whispered in her ear.

"What diet?" Belinda asked, overhearing me.

"Um..." April hesitated.

Before she could say anymore, her father appeared, smoking a cigarette.

"Joe, put that cigarette out," Belinda fussed.

I was grateful because with us finding out about April's pregnancy, I didn't need her inhaling anything.

"Hey, Daddy." April hugged her father.

Joe returned her hug. "When did you two get here?"

"Just," April replied, releasing her father to help Belinda set up lunch as she carried the plates to the table.

"Mr. Kevin. How's the hospital world doing?" Joe queried.

"I lost a patient, unfortunately. Hanging tough with your daughter's help."

"Daphne told me you guys got back together," Belinda commented.

"Yes, and we're living together. Oh, and I'm pregnant," April announced.

Belinda dropped a plate, and it smashed on the floor.

"Congratulations, baby. I'm happy for you." Joe beamed.

"Thanks, Daddy," April muttered, fidgeting with her hands.

"When's the wedding?" Belinda demanded.

April thought I wasn't ready to get married again and was worried I only wanted her as a baby mother. But I had plans to one day change her last name. Her mother made demands on her, but we followed our own rules.

"Ma, we just found out I'm pregnant. Let me ease into that part before you throw a wedding."

"I'm sure Kevin's parents are thinking the same thing. You two can't go around being just baby momma and baby daddies. That child should be born with a united couple," Belinda chastised, nostrils flared as she pointed between us.

Joe shook his head at her. "Belinda, leave these kids alone. They can figure things out for themselves." He picked up a fork and took a bite of his fish.

April smiled gratefully. "Thank you, Daddy,"

"That's her problem. You've always spoiled her, Joe," Belinda sneered.

"Mrs. Benson, I promise April and our child will never come second to anyone. My family is the most important thing to me. The life we've created will be loved by two people who love each other," I said, lifting April's hand and kissing her knuckles.

"Remember those words when he dumps you for someone else in nine months. You should've stayed with the other guy who wanted to marry you," Belinda said.

"Hush, Belinda!" Joe shouted.

The room went completely silent. April looked ready to walk out the door, but I slid my hand over her thigh and squeezed, letting her know I was there and we'd be okay.

Chapter 27

April

Two weeks after dinner with my parents, I was less stressed and working fewer hours. My mother and I talked on the phone afterward, and she apologized for her behavior. She told me she loved me no matter what and understood that I had to live my own life.

Kevin was on his way home, so I helped Ella with her homework in the kitchen while we waited for dinner. I wanted tonight to be special and see how Ella felt about having a little brother or sister join the family. I'd spoken to Kevin's mom on the phone earlier, and she told me all his favorite foods: steak, pasta, shrimp stir-fry, and chocolate cake. I even picked up a little outfit for later when Ella went to bed and we were alone.

"April, can I ask you a question and not get in trouble?" Ella asked.

I wiped my hands on the dishrag. "You can ask me anything, little nugget." Sitting beside her at the table, I ran a finger across her drawing of her dad and mom.

"Can I call you Mommy? I don't want Daddy to feel bad, but I like having you around."

"Why would you think he would feel bad, sweetie?"

"I don't want you to break up and not get to see you anymore. My friend Kaila's parents are getting divorced."

"You never have to worry about not seeing me, and I would be honored to be your bonus mom."

"Pinky swear?" Ella asked, holding out her pinky finger. I entwined our hands, and we did our brief secret handshake.

The door opened, and Kevin walked in with a bag of groceries. "Look at my gorgeous girls. You miss me?" He kissed Ella's forehead before dropping a kiss on my lips. Dropping the bag on the counter, he started putting things away.

I looked at Ella. "How about you go and wash up before dinner?"

Ella nodded and ran toward the bathroom in the hallway. I smiled, loving the bond we'd created.

"What are you cooking, baby?" Kevin asked, lifting the lids on the pots on the stove.

"Your favorite. Steak, shrimp stir-fry, pasta, and chocolate cake. I have a good six-pack of beer chilling in the fridge. Afterward, you can have me for dessert unless the chocolate cake is enough." I stood on my tiptoes to kiss him.

He gripped my butt cheeks, taking the kiss further as he backed me against the counter. I moaned into his mouth before gently pushing him away. "Save that energy for later, Sir."

He groaned at my words, keeping me close. "How was Ella today? Did you girls do anything fun? I didn't get any alerts from American Express, so I guess you didn't spend all my money."

I loved being this close to him and talking about our day. "No, she was fine, and we mostly stayed in and watched movies." I kissed him lightly. "Go wash up, please. Dinner will be ready in five minutes."

I tilted my head, admiring his sexy ass in his scrubs as he left the kitchen. *Maybe we can play doctor and nurse tonight.*

A few minutes later, we were eating and laughing about our day.

"We wanted to talk to you about something, nugget," Kevin said, placing his napkin on the table.

Ella turned to look at him. "Okay."

"April and I are going to have a baby. Would you like to have a little sister or brother?"

Ella clapped her hands and cheered. "Yes! So cool! I get to be a big sister."

"You do, nugget," I replied.

"So you'll be their mom and my mom too?" Ella questioned.

I hadn't had the chance to mention our earlier conversation with Kevin. By the look on his face, her statement completely shocked him.

"Ella—"

"Ella, where did you get the idea to call April Mom?" Kevin cut me off before I could answer her question.

"I did, Daddy. Don't be mad at April and send her away. Kaila's parents aren't together anymore, and she doesn't see her dad much."

"I'm not mad, sweetheart. I didn't think to talk to you about April moving in with us. I'm glad you have someone you can talk to about certain things. She's not going anywhere. I can promise you that," Kevin said, looking at me.

I jumped up to grab dessert, but Kevin clasped my hand.

"Baby, before you grab dessert, I want to say something quick."

I nodded to go ahead with what he had to say.

Still holding my hand, he stood and then lowered to one knee. Tears pooled in my eyes as he pulled a small black box from his jogging pants.

"April, from the moment I met you. I knew I couldn't stay away from your rude attitude and sexy ass mouth," Kevin started to say, and I cackled.

"You said a dirty word, Daddy," Ella told him, holding her hand out for a dollar to put in the swear jar.

Kevin and I laughed as he pulled out his wallet and gave her a dollar.

"Like I was saying, I didn't think it was possible to fall in love again, let alone with someone who challenges me the way you do. You've accepted my baby girl, and now we're bringing a new life into the world. I fall more in love with you every day." Kevin took a deep breath, and his eyes were glued to mine. "April Benson, will you do me the honor of being my wife?"

"The moment I fell on top of you with the food tray, I knew we were in for a bumpy ride," I said, and we laughed at my comment. "These past few months have shown me a fresh vision and purpose I didn't think I was capable of. Falling in love with you was not in my plans, but I'm glad I did, and I get to spend the rest of my life with you and Ella. I would love to be your wife."

Kevin placed the ring on my finger and stood, cupping my face and kissing me softly. Ella wrapped her hands around us as we pulled apart, and he picked her up. The ring was half a carat, a gorgeous sparkling halo with beautiful scalloped pavé diamonds encircling the center.

"This ring is beautiful, Kevin."

He kissed me again. "Not as beautiful as you."

...

We gave Ella a bath after dinner and put her to bed. Once she was asleep, I asked Kevin if we could play. At first, he was hesitant, and I understood why. But I was early in my pregnancy and not even showing.

Our bedroom was lit with candles, and soft music played so we wouldn't wake Ella. I was flat on my back, lying on the bed with my legs spread wide. My ankles were tied to the bed, and my wrists were secured to the headboard. Kevin wore pajama pants that hung loosely off his hips, the thick imprint of his dick clearly visible. He admired me spread on the bed, and I was already wet thinking about what he would do to me.

"How are you feeling, baby? Are you up for this?" Kevin moved to the edge of the bed, running his hand across my ankle and up my thigh to stop at my belly.

"I feel fine, baby."

"What if we elope to Vegas like Warren and Kyla? I don't think I can take a long engagement," Kevin said, bending to slip his tongue in my mouth.

"Mmm... Ah," I moaned as his fingers entered my pussy slowly.

"I have another question, baby." He removed his fingers from my sex and slid them into his mouth. Opening the drawer of the nightstand, he pulled out a black box.

"You already proposed, baby. What else is there?" I wondered.

Kevin opened the box to reveal a black collar with gold and diamonds around the edges. He took the collar out of the box and sat on the bed next to me. I knew about this from Kyla. When you become a submissive, your Dom proposes with a collar especially for you.

Am I ready for this? Can I be a mother, a submissive wife, and a nurse?

Kevin stared into my eyes. "Would you do me the honor of wearing my collar, baby?"

I didn't know if I waited too long, but he suddenly stood and closed the box.

"Kevin, wait! Yes, I'd like to wear your collar and be fully committed to you."

"Are you sure? I don't want you to have regrets about me, us, or what this represents. We're equal in this relationship, and I would never do anything to hurt you," Kevin promised.

"Yes, Sir. I'm positive." I'd never be comfortable calling him "Master," and he respected my choice. I was new to this world, and Kevin had shown me things beyond my wildest dreams.

He smiled. "Then let's begin."

Kevin removed his pajama pants. He was fully erect, and my mouth watered, wanting to taste him. He climbed on the bed, caressing my thigh. Sliding his hands under my ass, he lined up his tongue with my sex, a smile tugging at his lips. "I'm going to fuck you until you pass out," he muttered right before he swiped his tongue over my sex.

"Yes!"

His grip tightened as he devoured me. It was his goal

to see me come undone under his touch. The flick of his thumb caused my wetness to seep onto the bedsheets. He dipped a second finger inside me, wetting it to spread the moistness around my clit.

"Kevin! Ah, fuck!"

"What's my name, baby?"

"Sir! Oh, God, Sir! Please, fuck me."

His tongue thrust in and out steadily as his thumb slid into my ass. We'd only practiced with butt plugs, but I hoped we'd move in that direction one day.

"Baby, you taste so good." Kevin removed his mouth from me and lined his erection up with my entrance. He eased the tip inside before pulling out again. "Fuck! You're choking my dick, baby," he huffed, tapping his shaft against my clit.

"Sir, I need to come."

"Not yet." He gripped my chin, coaxing my mouth open. His tongue plunged into my mouth as his dick entered me, causing me to lose all my senses.

He thrust in and out, gripping my hips as the slaps of our bodies coming together echoed in the room. An out-of-control storm raged inside him. He threw his head back, closed his eyes, and caressed my stomach lovingly. Our moans and grunts picked up, and the headboard started to shake as the cusp of our orgasms coiled to the surface.

"Oh! Right there. Keep going, please."

"You like that, baby, huh? Tell me you like it when I make love to you, fuck you, and please you."

"I love you!" I screamed out as we both came.

"Shit!" Kevin fell over me, still inside me, as he twitched and writhed.

He kissed me deeply, removing the ties from my

wrists and ankles, and pulled me into his arms. He kissed my forehead as sleep threatened to pull me under.

"Give me five minutes, and I'll be ready for round two, baby."

"This time, I choose the toy," I teased sleepily, peppering his face with kisses.

"Whatever makes you happy, baby?"

Epilogue: Kevin

Months later.

April was draped in a burgundy wrap dress and wore flat sandals. I watched her as she talked with Kyla, Lisa, Chasity, and the other women of Club Seek. I promised we'd go back after the baby was born.

Today, I'd thrown a barbeque to celebrate moving in together, our engagement, and pregnancy. I couldn't be happier after April accepted my pendant two months ago. My life was so different compared to a year ago. I knew Aaliyah would be happy I'd found happiness again, and Ella would have someone she could count on to keep her spirit alive and raise her with love and care.

"I see that look in your eye, bro." Warren smirked.

"What look?" I replied, taking a swig of the beer.

The food was cooked and laid out on the table. Ella was running around enjoying her friends and family. The kids had a bouncy house and a pool while the adults were set up for card games. Music blasted in the corner by the photo booth I'd rented.

My mom had made coleslaw, pies, spaghetti, and her

famous chocolate and strawberry cupcakes. April was also a superb cook, and she'd helped with the pasta salad, baked beans, and mac and cheese. I appreciated her letting my mom know we still needed her in Ella's life.

"You're ready for the party to be over so you can take your woman upstairs and play," Warren joked.

I chuckled. It was true, and sharing her with everyone for the next few hours was cutting into my time. Call me selfish, but April had opened me up to love again, and I refused to let anyone or anything get in our way.

Ella ran over to April, and she scooped her up. I told April she shouldn't pick her up anymore now she was pregnant.

I placed my beer on the table as she walked toward me, kissing her cheek as I took Ella from her arms. "Little nugget, how many times have I told you that April can't pick you up anymore?" I kissed her little fingers, pretending to eat them.

Ella giggled and squirmed, wanting to get down. "Daddy, Mommy said it was okay. Right, Mommy April?"

"That's right, Ella. Your dad just worries about your little sister. You didn't hurt me, sweetie," April responded, kissing her forehead.

I watched as Ella ran off toward the other kids in the pool, pulling April close for a kiss.

"You better stop before you get something started out here," April whined, trying to wiggle out of my hold.

"You two will end up pregnant again within a year," Kyla said, laughing.

April moved out of my reach. "No, ma'am, don't put that on me. This is my one and only child."

I chuckled, sliding my arm around her shoulder and

pulling her close again. "What if I do that thing you like with my tongue? Can I have another baby then?"

April nodded, biting her lip as she wrapped her arm around my waist.

"I'm feeling a little tired. April, can you come and rub my back for me?" I asked.

Everyone burst into laughter.

"We already know you're not coming back out. Don't fake it, brother," Warren teased, holding Kyla in his arms.

My hand eased around April's waist, squeezing her gently. "What can I say? She's in a safe place."

* * *

I hope you enjoyed April and Kevin's story. Check out the **"Seeking in Romance"** series, filled with a host of characters mentioned. https://books2read.com/u/4ELGLe

Follow up with "Tease Me," cigar bar, book club, interconnected standalones. The next book in the series, **"Promise Me,"** is a forbidden, age-gap romance https://books2read.com/u/mB5nRA

Have you checked out **"His Peace Her Pleasure?"** Click here: https://books2read.com/u/3JJroP, a billionaire, steamy romance.

Also, steamy romance that includes bodyguards, one-night stands, **"Protecting Yanira"** https://books2read.com/u/bzBrAZ

Don't forget, if you love fling romances, bodyguards, and forced proximity, check out **"Protecting Chanel"** https://books2read.com/u/mqwPB8

If you love brother's best friend romance, you'll love

"Sensual" here: https://books2read.com/u/49lYYM with a dash of steamy romance.

Check out Bodyguard Romance, military, romantic suspense here ***Protecting Bria.***

https://books2read.com/u/bQJkjd

Follow college romance and more characters in *"**Taste**"* here: https://books2read.com/u/bpz1Ng

Please also check out ***"Love Don't Live Here Anymore Vanessa Andrew."***

https://books2read.com/u/mBOWGZ a steamy curvy girl, enemies to lovers romance.

Follow that up with a workplace vacation romance in **"Love Don't Live Here Anymore Isabella Andrew."** https://books2read.com/u/brVNO7

More workplace, boss romances with **"Love by Design Boxset 1-3."** https://books2read.com/u/m2ldEk

About the Author

A TENNESSEE NATIVE and California dreaming Author KeKe Renée, is living and striving to continue her passion for writing short story romances in genres ranging from Erotic, Paranormal, and Women's Fiction.

Playlist

1. Janet Jackson—Rope Burn
2. Beyonce—Haunted
3. FKA Twigs—Papi Pacify
4. D'Angelo—How Does It Feel
5. Chris Brown—Fuck You Back to Sleep
6. Jeremiah—Fuck You All the Time
7. Rihanna—Higher
8. Ella Mai—Shot Clock
9. Silk—Freak Me

What's Next

304 Publishing Company

We showcase authors writing African American, Interracial, Women's Fiction, Urban Romance, Erotic, and Contemporary Romance novels. Along with Mystery, Thriller, Suspense, Poetry, Beauty, and Style Books. Thank you for taking the time out to visit. Join our mailing list to stay updated with new releases and blog posts.

Catalog Releases

- Wet Heat (Wet Heat Series Book 1)
- Every time We Touch Novelette (Wet Heat Book 2 Series)
- His Peace, Her Pleasure
- Baby, It's Cold Outside
- Love Don't Live Here Anymore, Vanessa Andrew Book 1
- Love Don't Live Here Anymore, Isabella Andrew Book 2
- One Night Only-A Novelette (Love by Design Book 1)
- Cassian and Savannah (Love by Design Book 2)
- Deidra's Love (Love by Design Book 3)
- Protecting Bria (Special Force Operation Alphas)
- Protecting Chanel (Special Force Operation Alphas)
- Haven
- Taste (A New Adult romance)
- Sensual
- Seek To Please
- Seek To Bare

•Seek To Touch
•Seek To Love
•Seek To Trust
•Seek To Earn
•Protecting Yanira (Special Force Operation Alphas)

Thank you so much for reading. If you enjoyed the crazy ride and want to leave a review, we'd truly appreciate the support.

Acknowledgments

I CAN'T MENTION ENOUGH the support and dedication of my author buddies for keeping me uplifted. My behind-the-scenes team of beta readers, editors, designers, and more. As a writer, I continue to strive for the best, and I appreciate each and every person who reads my work. Without your continual feedback, I wouldn't be on this path, letting doubts slip away.

9 781955 233491